BEGINNINGS BY THE SEA

AN OAK ISLAND NOVEL
BOOK 2

L.P. DOVER

Beginnings by the Sea (An Oak Island Novel)
Copyright 2023 by L.P. Dover
Edited by: Yvette Rebello at YR Editor
Cover Designed by: Letitia Hasser at RBA Designs

❁ Created with Vellum

OAK ISLAND SERIES

Hide Away by the Sea
Beginnings by the Sea

More to come!

1

NYLA

The salty scent of the ocean breeze wafted through the air, ruffling my hair as I locked the door to the new home I'd lived in for the past seven months. Even though seven months wasn't that long, the quaint town of Oak Island already felt like home. I came here to seek a fresh start; it was the best decision I'd ever made.

"Good morning, Dr. Clark!" a voice shouted across the street.

A smile lit up my face and a blast of warmth spread through my chest. Turning around, I waved at my elderly neighbor and walked down the front porch steps to my red Jeep Wrangler.

"Good morning, George," I hollered back.

He and his wife had lived in their little white house across the street all fifty-eight years of their marriage. George picked up his newspaper off the ground, and I could tell by the wince on his face that it hurt to straighten his stance. But still, he smiled at me and waved.

"Heading to the office?"

I nodded. "Yep. I'm starting to think you might need to visit me. That back of yours is giving you some problems, right?"

George waved the newspaper dismissively in the air. "Young lady, when you get as old as me, there isn't a day when you don't feel aches or pains. It's a sign that I've lived my life to the fullest."

That made me laugh. "I'll have to remember that." I waved again. "Have a good day, George. Tell Rose I said hello and that the lemon cookies she made me the other day are all gone."

George chuckled. "She'll be happy to hear it."

He slowly walked to the door, and I ensured he got inside before climbing into my Jeep. While on my way to work, a pang of sadness washed over me as I thought about George and Rose moving up in age. I haven't known them long, but I knew we were all on borrowed time, especially them. None of my grandparents were alive; I lost my last grandfather four years ago to congestive heart failure; he was eighty-two. Sadly, the other three grandparents I had all passed away in their sixties or early seventies, leaving an unbearable void in my family tree. My mom also lost two of her younger sisters to cancer. That was one of the reasons why I decided to go to medical school. I wanted to learn more about how our bodies work and how to heal people. Granted, I didn't have the knowledge to cure cancer, but if I could help a person's health in any way, that was good enough for me.

When I arrived at the office, it was precisely seven forty-five. One of the nurses who worked for me, Autumn Collins, pulled in right behind me in her silver Honda Accord. She parked beside me and when she looked over, she had the biggest grin on her face.

I grabbed my purse and hopped out of my car. "Why are you so happy this morning?" I asked, joining her so we could walk into the clinic together.

She had on her Carolina blue scrubs just like me, but hers matched her eyes perfectly. My blue eyes were a shade darker, and I'd always been told it was rare for someone with red hair to have the color of eyes I did. Autumn shouldered her purse and quickly wrapped her long, bright blonde hair into a messy bun on top of her head as we walked. She made it look so effortless. Whenever I tried to do the same thing with my hair, it always looked like a rat's nest.

"I'm happy," she said, grinning at me, "because it's Friday and the weather is going to be perfect this weekend."

I unlocked the back door and waved a hand for her to go in. "Do you have plans with anyone special?" I asked her.

She snorted and glanced at me over her shoulder. "I wouldn't exactly call it that," she replied, stopping by the lab and flipping on the light. "He's just an old friend from high school. When he heard I moved back here, he called."

"Ah, I see," I said, smirking as I walked past her to my office. She stopped at my door, leaning her shoulder against the frame. I turned on my light and set my purse on my desk. "It must be nice coming back here after years of being away and still having friends."

Autumn smiled. "It is, but it's been great making new ones, too. I'm thrilled you hired me."

"Me too," I replied in all honesty.

Autumn was twenty-eight years old, which was four years younger than me. She'd graduated from UNC Charlotte with a nursing degree and stayed there for a few years with some of her fellow nursing friends. But in the end, she missed home and wanted to move back to Oak Island. I couldn't blame her. If I'd known how amazing Oak Island was before, I would've left Boston in a heartbeat.

Luckily, I had my best friend and partner at Seaside Family Practice, Dr. Everleigh McLean, to thank for that. It was because of her I was able to begin anew. Everleigh's father retired and she offered to take over the practice.

When she offered me a partnership, I didn't hesitate to answer yes. Never in a million years did I imagine having my own practice. I'd been an ER doctor at Massachusetts General for years. My life was a chaotic mess, always on the go. Now I could breathe and enjoy life at a slower pace; it was heaven.

The bell to the front door jingled and I could hear Gina's voice as she sang her favorite Celine Dion song.

Autumn snickered and shook her head. "That woman is something else. Don't get me wrong, I love Celine Dion, but she comes in like that *every* morning."

Gina's singing grew louder until she appeared behind Autumn, her smile bright as she patted Autumn on the shoulder and looked in on me. She wore a set of light purple scrubs that encased her petite frame and contrasted with her short black hair. Her glasses were perched atop her nose, the bright purple frames complementing her outfit. Gina was fifty-eight years old and was looking for a job after being let go from the library. Everleigh's mother used to handle the practice's front desk until she retired along with Everleigh's father, leaving the position open.

"Good morning," she said cheerily. "Looks like a busy day; we've got a lot of possible sinus infections here due to all the pollen." She glanced over at Autumn. "Should I call Janie in to help?"

Autumn shook her head. "No need. We'll be fine."

Janie usually worked as Everleigh's nurse but had been helping around the office since Everleigh was taking time off before her baby boy was due. On busier days, having two nurses made things easier.

I looked at Autumn skeptically. "Are you sure you can handle it?"

A smirk formed on her lips. "Please. I'm more worried about you."

This was met by a chuckle from Gina, who quickly turned on her heel. "Going to make coffee now. You're both going to need it."

I grabbed the stethoscope off my desk and draped it around my neck. "All right, let's get this day started," I told Autumn.

We walked down the hall to the front desk, and a couple of patients were already in the waiting room. While Gina checked them in, I stood back with Autumn in the hallway.

"Are you excited about the festival coming up?" Autumn asked.

A groan escaped my lips. Even though I was doing it for a good cause, it still made me nervous. "I can't believe you and Everleigh came up with it and I agreed," I grumbled, hanging my head.

Autumn giggled and nudged me with her elbow. "Hey, we were just trying to help. You're single and this town is full of eligible men who'd love to take a hot doctor out on a date."

Since moving into town, I'd met several men, but

it was hard to focus on dating when I was trying to get used to my new life. A part of me knew I was ready to date, and I think Everleigh and Autumn knew it, too. That was why they did what they did.

The Oak Island Spring Festival was happening in just a little over a month—which seemed like a long time, but it really wasn't—where tons of vendors set up booths to showcase their work. There was going to be music, food, and hundreds of giveaways and prizes. It just so happened that Everleigh signed us up to draw more people to our practice with our special prize . . . a date with a doctor. That was what she was calling it. She even had a giant poster made with a picture of me on it which she planned on sitting at our booth. I only agreed to do it if the money went to charity.

Thankfully, it wasn't a romantic date; it was just for two hours at the local ice cream shop once the festival ended.

"What if no one buys a ticket?" I said, looking over at Autumn. "That'll be so embarrassing."

Autumn turned to face me and placed her hands on my shoulders. "Are you serious? I know of six guys already who want to enter."

The breath hitched in my lungs. "Who? Why haven't you told me this?"

Autumn winked, her bright blue eyes twinkling. "Don't worry. You'll see soon enough."

Gina brought Autumn our first patient's chart,

and Autumn snickered as she walked away. Was I ready to move on with my life? The pain and hurt from my divorce still lingered like a shadow in my heart, even though it had been almost three years since then. A twinge of pain sparked in my chest, but I shook it off, pushing away the sadness that threatened to resurface. It was time to forget the past and move on. *I can do this.*

2

NYLA

"How are things at the office? Do you miss me yet?" Everleigh asked, her bright hazel-green eyes dancing as she lifted her glass of homemade lemonade to take a sip.

She looked so cute and motherly in her pale green maternity top that flowed over her belly. Even her caramel-blonde hair seemed brighter; it had to be the pregnancy glow. I pressed my fingertips against my chest and lightly rested my other hand on her arm.

"Oh yes, desperately," I said sarcastically. "I don't know how I keep our office running without you."

Everleigh laughed and tossed a sweet potato fry into her mouth. "Okay, now. That's not how you're supposed to say it. I was hoping you really did miss me."

I smiled warmly and gave her arm a gentle

squeeze. "You know I do. Why do you think we meet here at The Beachcomber twice a week on top of our usual Tuesday tradition since you stopped working?" I asked, waving a hand about the small but cozy restaurant with its beachy décor —exposed lightbulbs, driftwood signs, and surfboards hanging from the wall. "That's three times a week, Everleigh," I laughed. "But hey, if you want to see me more, maybe we can add an afternoon girls' date to the bakery. We can meet Michelle and Trish there and grab some chocolate cake pops."

Michelle and Trish were Everleigh's friends who she introduced me to before I even decided to move to Oak Island. They were married to two of her husband's friends. Now they were all my friends, and they never treated me as an outsider. Every Tuesday night, the big group of us would meet at this same spot and have dinner. It was a tradition I looked forward to every week, even if I was the seventh wheel. All of them were happily married. There was a time when I thought I would be, but I screwed that up.

Everleigh rubbed her pregnant belly and closed her eyes. "Chocolate cake pops sound amazing right now. I blame Michelle for the last ten pounds I've gained."

We both laughed and I nodded, glad to get my thoughts away from my past. "Yeah, I need to have some words with her, too. I think I've put on five because of them; it's all her fault."

"Hey, ladies," Debbie greeted as she poured more ice water into my glass.

Debbie Carroll was the owner of The Beachcomber. She was fifty-eight years old and a tiny lady with tanned skin from loving the sun, with chin-length dark hair that was always wavy.

"Thank you, Debbie," I said, lifting my glass of water.

She winked at me and draped an arm around Everleigh's shoulder with the biggest grin on her face. "Guess what I'm cooking Tuesday night for you."

I clutched my stomach. "Please tell me it's mahi mahi."

Debbie chuckled. "Yep. I know you girls love it."

Everleigh patted Debbie's hand that rested on her shoulder. "We love you, Debs. We can't wait."

Debbie smiled again and then left us to walk around the restaurant. I finished the last bite of my pan-seared salmon and stole a sweet potato fry from Everleigh's plate. She tilted her head back and laughed.

"Why do you always steal my fries? You know you can order some."

I shrugged. "Yeah, but then I'd eat all of them."

Everleigh snickered and ate the last one off her plate. "I know the feeling. They're too good not to."

Her eyes widened and she gasped. "Oh, I forgot to ask about your parents. How did their three-week trip to Greece go? They just got back, right?"

Grinning, I reached into my purse for my phone, filled with a million pictures my mom sent just last night. I passed it to her so she could see them.

"They had a blast," I said, looking at the photos as she scrolled. "They've been married fifty years."

The Greece trip was their anniversary present to each other. Everleigh shook her head in astonishment. "Fifty years. That's a long time. I'm hoping Jensen and I live long enough for that. We'll be in our eighties if we do."

She handed my cell back to me and I smiled. "I'm sure you will. Maybe I'll find my true love by then."

Everleigh scoffed. "If I have anything to say about it, you'll find Mr. Right very soon."

I rolled my eyes. "Auctioning me off at the spring festival for a date is not how to do it, my dear friend."

Everleigh laughed and shrugged playfully. "It's getting you out there, Nyla," she insisted. "Besides, I think it'll be fun. I can't wait to see all the men who enter. They'll be giving their hard-earned money toward one of your charities."

That was the only thing getting me through it. I could suffer through two hours of awkwardness for that. Then again, maybe I would get lucky, and the winner be a handsome man around my age.

I lifted my glass of water and took a sip. "Yeah, I guess it could be fun. What are friends for, right? I know you're trying to help."

Everleigh smirked. "Exactly. I found my happiness, and it's time you found yours."

"You've already done so much," I claimed, setting my glass down. "I wouldn't be half-owner of Seaside Family Practice if it wasn't for you."

Everleigh reached over and grabbed my hands. "It's the best decision I ever made. That's what friends do for each other."

Visions of the first time we met flashed through my mind. It was a little over two years ago at Massachusetts General Hospital where we both worked. My divorce had just been finalized and I was a mess. I didn't have much time left on my break, so I ran into the cafeteria, trying to get my food, when I slipped on a pile of peach cobbler on the floor. Everleigh was the one who helped me up; we'd been friends ever since. I couldn't stop from smiling at all the memories.

"What are you thinking about?" Everleigh asked, cocking her head to the side.

"The first time we met," I replied.

She slapped a hand over her mouth. "Oh yeah, the peach cobbler. I'll never forget that."

I laughed. "Neither will I. And speaking of cobbler, do we want to grab dessert here or go to the bakery?"

Sighing, Everleigh glanced down at her empty plate. "You are seriously a bad influence on me." Her gaze lifted to mine and a devilish grin spread across her face. "Fine. Let's go to the bakery." Reaching into my purse, I grabbed my credit card out of my wallet and stood. "Wait," Everleigh called out, holding up a hand. "Isn't it my turn to pay?"

I shook my head. "Nope. It's mine. I think the pregnancy hormones are messing with your memory."

Technically, it *was* her time to pay, and she realized it just as I hurried off to the bar before she could argue with me. Evie was behind the bar working on drink orders, dressed in a pink tank top with The Beachcomber logo on it; she was also Debbie's twenty-three-year-old daughter and looked exactly like her, except her dark hair wasn't short like her mother's. It was long and wavy down her back, almost making her look like a mermaid.

The Beachcomber was going to be Evie's one day when Debbie retired. However, I didn't see that time coming anytime soon. Debbie was a people person and loved being involved with the restaurant. Evie watched me hurry to the counter and smiled as she shook her head.

"I was just about to set the check on your table. You didn't have to come up here."

I waved a hand dismissively in the air. "No

worries. I thought I'd save you the trouble. You guys are slammed today."

Then again, it was lunchtime on a Saturday, so that made sense. Evie took my card and glanced over my shoulder to who I could only assume was Everleigh.

"Isn't it Everleigh's turn to pay?" she asked, focusing back on me and then over at Everleigh again. "Because she's shaking her head at me and giving me the evil eye."

"Just run my card," I said, grinning over my shoulder at Everleigh, who scowled half-heartedly at me. "She'll get over it," I reiterated to Evie as I faced her again.

Evie giggled. "You guys are too funny. She won't let you get away with it next time," she said, running my card through the machine and handing me the receipt. I signed my name and added a hefty tip.

"Oh, I know. Everleigh is one stubborn woman."

Evie nodded in agreement. "That she is. You two have a good rest of the weekend. I'll see you and the rest of the crew on Tuesday."

She smiled and moved down the bar, her hips swaying in tune to the music that filled the air, as she headed to a group of guys who wanted a round of beer. Evie was a social butterfly, just like her mother. She seemed so at ease at talking to people she didn't even know.

When I was twenty-three, I was the same way. I met people everywhere and had numerous dates lined up for the weekends. At least until I met my ex-husband, Miles. He was everything I ever wanted, and it was effortless at the beginning of our relationship. We got along great, could talk for hours, and never ran out of things to say. The passion and desire between us were off the charts. Sadly, I let my career get in the way, breaking us apart. I haven't experienced a relationship like I had with Miles with anyone else since then.

Now that I was thirty-two, things didn't feel as easy anymore. Guess you could say I was out of practice when it came to dating.

I took one last look at the receipt to ensure I added the tip right. Once I confirmed I did my math correctly, I turned quickly and bumped right into a man who clasped my arms in his firm yet gentle grasp.

"Whoa, easy there," he said, chuckling lightly.

The impact caught me off guard and I gasped. "I am so sorry," I apologized, lifting my gaze from the man's broad chest to his face.

He was handsome and perfectly coifed with his gelled dark hair and polo shirt that matched his forest green eyes. I'd been living in Oak Island for months, but if I had to guess, the man wasn't a local. Judging by the smell of his expensive cologne and the several thousand-dollar watch on his wrist, I'd say he was probably from a big city. New York would be my guess.

The man grinned and let me go, his smile warm and inviting. "There's no need to apologize," he said, stepping back. "I shouldn't have been so close." He held out his hand. "My name's Cohen."

I shook his hand. "Nyla."

His grip was firm and I liked it.

"Are you from around here, or are you visiting?" he asked.

I happened to look over at Everleigh, and she wore a big smile while discreetly waving her hand like she was urging me to talk to the guy.

"I live here in Oak Island," I replied, focusing back on Cohen. "And you?" I wondered, trailing my gaze over his pricey clothes and shoes.

Cohen noticed what I was doing and chuckled. "Actually, I just moved here from New York a couple of weeks ago. I've been a little busy with work, but now that things are settled, I've had some time to get out." I couldn't stop the smile that spread across my face. Cohen's gaze narrowed curiously, and he grinned wider. "Why are you smiling?"

I shook my head. "I figured you were from one of the big cities up north."

He smirked knowingly. "What gave me away?"

I shrugged. "I'm from Boston. I can spot a city guy from a mile away."

"Ah, so you don't hold the title of local either, do you?" he said.

"Yes, she does," Evie chimed in from down the bar. "And I think she fits in perfectly."

Debbie happened to walk by and patted me on the shoulder. "I second that," she replied in passing.

Cohen chuckled and shook his head. "Okay, so you're a local now. I would love to be considered one too one day. Do you think you could give me some tips on how to fit in?" He nodded at the bar. "I can buy you a drink and we talk about it?"

My stomach fluttered with excitement. The man was charming, but I would say no even if I didn't have plans with Everleigh. The last thing I wanted was to appear too eager.

"I'm sorry," I told him. "But I'm here with a friend and we have plans today. Maybe some other time?"

Cohen stepped out of the way and nodded. "I'd like that. Hopefully, I'll see you around town."

I shrugged. "It's possible."

Pulse racing, I walked past him, trying not to grin like an idiot as I returned to Everleigh. She stood and handed me my purse, her eyes flicking back and forth from me to Cohen, who sat down at the bar.

"He is charming," Everleigh whispered. "I recognize him from an article in our town's paper the other day."

My mouth gaped and I blinked in surprise. "What? What for?"

She snickered. "He's a local hero. Why do you think I was waving for you to talk to him?"

I shrugged. "I don't know . . . because he's hot?"

Everleigh rolled her eyes. "Well, yes, there's that, but he's also a big-time businessman savvy with his money. He just bought out Freddy's Surf Shop and saved the Absher family from going bankrupt. The wintertime hit Freddy hard, and he couldn't recoup." She nodded over at Cohen. "This guy restructured everything, and now Freddy's shop has had triple sales this week alone. Granted, he had to sell, but Freddy can buy everything back when the store starts bringing in more money. It's a win-win if it works out."

I was impressed.

My gaze drifted over to Cohen, watching him talk amiably with Debbie as if they were lifelong friends. At least I knew something good about the newcomer.

"Are you ready to get some cake pops?" Everleigh asked.

Grinning, I turned to her. "Yep, let's go."

As we exited the restaurant and into the warm evening air, excitement bubbled inside me like champagne fizzing in a flute.

Would I see Cohen again?

God, I hoped so.

*I*t was a typical Monday at the office; nothing exciting happened except for a patient who pulled a muscle in his back as a result of trying to be adventurous with his wife. The man held nothing back, and it took all I had to keep a straight face the entire time he explained his story. Seeing older couples trying to keep the passion in their marriage was nice. Unfortunately, that was something I failed at. My ex-husband and I had the passion; I just didn't have the time.

"Someone's deep in thought," Autumn teased, her voice pulling me back to the here and now.

Grinning, I grabbed my purse from the bottom drawer on my desk and looked over at her standing in my office doorway. She'd already taken down her blonde hair and changed out of her scrubs into jeans and a light pink T-shirt.

Her smile broadened. "I still can't believe you didn't burst out laughing today while talking to Mr. Sheffield."

I raised my brows. "And I can't believe you were by the door listening the entire time."

Autumn held a hand over her mouth and laughed. "I couldn't help it. That man and his wife are seriously kinky. It's not every day we get something like that in our office. I want to be like them when I get old."

Shaking my head, I chuckled and slung my purse strap over my shoulder. "I'm sure you will. You just need to find a guy with the same kind of energy you have, someone who can keep up with you." I walked up to her. "With how outgoing and beautiful you are, I'm surprised you didn't go into acting. I could definitely see you being in movies."

Autumn's eyes lit up. "Trust me, I would've loved to have done something like that. Drama class was my favorite in high school; I starred in all the plays." Her smile faded slightly. "But unfortunately, getting noticed by talent agents isn't easy in a small town, and I didn't have the money to move to California."

I draped an arm around her shoulders as we walked down the hallway toward the back door. "If you had, I never would've met you. I'm sorry, but I'm happy you're working for me."

Autumn bumped me with her hip. "So am I. I love being a nurse."

I opened the back door for her, and she walked out. I was going to follow her, but couldn't find my cell in my purse when I reached in for it. Autumn waited for me, but I waved for her to go.

"I think I left my phone in the office. I'll see you tomorrow."

Autumn waved and opened the door to her silver Honda Accord. "See ya! Have a good night!"

Turning on my heel, I went back inside to my office and found my phone on the desk. The sound of shuffling papers caught my attention, so I went to the front desk to find Gina straightening things up. She was supposed to have left ten minutes ago.

"Don't you have a dinner date with your husband tonight?" I called out, making her jump with a hand to her chest.

She let out a gasp and laughed but then quickly pushed her chair under the desk. "I do. That's why I'm trying to hurry. You know I can't leave a messy desk." That was one of the things I loved about her; she was organized.

I chuckled. "Yeah, I know. But at least you look gorgeous. That should help with you showing up late."

She had on a bright yellow sundress and her makeup was spot on.

Gina snorted and stopped at the front door. "It better. I spent an extra thirty minutes getting ready this morning."

I motioned toward the door. "Get out of here before it gets even later. I'll lock up behind you and leave through the back."

Gina quickly pulled out her car keys. "Thanks, Dr. Clark. I'll see you in the morning."

As soon as she opened the door, a familiar face greeted us and I smiled as the man walked up the stairs, only it quickly vanished when I noticed the bloody towel pressed to his left side.

"Cohen, what happened?" I asked, pushing the door open wider.

His eyes widened with recognition when he saw me. When I met him at the restaurant the other day, I never told him I was a doctor. Cohen winced when he moved the towel away, but then a dashing grin took over. He looked different today, not as polished in fancy clothes. This time, he was dressed in jeans and a gray T-shirt that was blood-stained and ripped. I could see the gash on his side.

Cohen pressed the towel back to his body. "Nyla. What are you doing here?"

I nodded to my right where the wooden sign with mine and Everleigh's name was nailed to the building.

Cohen's gaze shifted to it and he laughed. "Ah, I see. You're the doctor."

Gina placed a gentle hand on my arm. "He looks like he's really hurt, Dr. Clark. What do you want to do?"

"You," I said, ushering her out the door, "are leaving. Go and enjoy your night. I can handle everything from here."

Gina's lips pursed. "Are you sure?"

Nodding, I motioned for her to leave. "I'm positive." She was hesitant to go but eventually walked down to her car parked out front. I stepped out of the way so Cohen could go inside. "Come on. Tell me what happened."

Cohen sighed and walked in, and I locked the door behind us. He moved the towel away and lifted his shirt so I could see the wound. The gash wasn't too deep, but it was long enough that he'd need a few stitches.

"It was clumsiness, really," Cohen confessed, lowering his tattered shirt. "I was on the roof of my house and slipped. There must've been a nail sticking out that got me when I tumbled down."

My mouth gaped as I stared right into his green eyes. "Did you actually fall off the roof, or were you able to stop yourself?"

Cohen chuckled. "I was able to stop, thank God." He peered around the room. "I remembered seeing this office when I drove through town the other day. I thought I could get here before you closed." With a heavy sigh, he met my eyes again. "I'm sorry for coming in like this. I can come back tomorrow during working hours."

I flourished a hand toward the door that led past

the front desk and to the exam rooms beyond. "No. You're getting help now. I want you to go down the hallway to the first door on the left. I'll be there in a minute; I have to grab a few things."

He did as I said, and I walked past the room to the lab where most of our supplies were. Once I had everything I needed loaded onto my tray, I went back to Cohen and tried my best not to stare at him as he sat on the exam table. He'd taken off his shirt, revealing his perfectly chiseled chest.

I cleared my throat and tried to focus on the task at hand. "Okay, let's get you cleaned up." I dabbed the wound with antiseptic and watched as Cohen winced. "Sorry about that," I said, trying to keep my hands steady.

"It's fine," he replied, his voice low and husky. "You're doing a great job."

I tried to ignore the heat rising to my cheeks and focused on stitching up the wound. Cohen winced a few more times, but he was tough and insisted on me not using an anesthetic. I was shocked, especially since he was a city boy from New York. But, I had to say, he reminded me of Patrick Swayze in *Road House* when his character, Dalton, was slashed with a knife in a bar fight and he refused anesthetic when the main female lead, who was a doctor, tried to stitch him up. The whole scenario reminded me of that scene. I never thought I'd ever have a patient that would live up to Dalton's standards. It turned out Cohen didn't disappoint.

As I finished placing the bandage over the wound, I couldn't help but admire his physique. He was tall, with broad shoulders and defined biceps. Once I removed my gloves, Cohen's hand was on mine, interrupting my thoughts.

"Thank you," he said, his voice soft.

"You're welcome," I replied, feeling a little breathless.

As I pulled my hand away, I couldn't help but feel a fluttering sensation in my chest as I looked into Cohen's eyes. There was something familiar about him, but I couldn't place it. It was almost like déjà vu.

Cohen cleared his throat, breaking the silence. "You know," he said, sliding off the exam table, "I was hoping I'd run into you again."

I smiled. "Same."

His brows lifted. "Well, in that case, could you let me pay you back for seeing me after hours?"

Excitement coursed through me. "What did you have in mind?"

His gaze drifted down to my lips, and he smirked when his eyes lifted back to mine. "Dinner . . . tonight?"

My stomach fluttered in so many different ways as I thought about what this date could lead to. I didn't want to say no, but I also knew that getting close to someone would open me up to heartache; it was inevitable.

Was it a risk I was willing to take? You better believe it.

Cohen's smile widened and he chuckled. "What do you say, Nyla? Will you go out to dinner with me tonight?"

There was no hesitation in my voice when I answered. "Yes," I said. "Just tell me where and I'll be there."

hen Cohen left the office, I rushed home and rummaged through my closet. I finally settled on a short black dress that hugged my curves in all the right places, and slipped on a pair of strappy silver heels.

I combed my long red hair so it cascaded down my back in gentle waves. Cohen offered to take me anywhere I wanted to go, and since I was meeting Everleigh and the rest of our friends at The Beachcomber tomorrow, I didn't want to choose there. Plus, it was where most of the locals went, and I didn't want to draw attention to myself yet. Word traveled fast in small towns, and Cohen was already widely known. The last thing I wanted was for my patients to come in and ask questions about my love life. That was why I decided on Tranquil Island Bistro; it was just outside of town.

Cohen wanted to pick me up for our date, but I opted to drive myself . . . at least for our first one. I'd learned that lesson the hard way. Nothing was worse than being stuck on a horrible date with no escape. But, in all honesty, I didn't foresee mine and Cohen's dinner turning out that way. He seemed like a good guy, and from what I'd read about him in the town news article, he was very successful and respected.

I arrived at Tranquil Island Bistro at 7:30 p.m. sharp. The sun had set, and the restaurant was illuminated by twinkling fairy lights strung around the outdoor patio.

As I exited my car, I saw Cohen standing by the entrance, looking handsome in his black suit and white shirt. He smiled as he saw me approaching, and I felt butterflies in my stomach.

"You look beautiful," he said, reaching for my hand.

"Thank you," I replied, feeling my cheeks flush. "You look mighty fine yourself."

I loved the way he had his hair gelled to where it was sort of messy but not. His suit was tailored to perfection, fitting the exact contours of his muscles. The top two buttons of his white shirt were undone, exposing his smooth, tanned skin. I had no doubt there was a set of chiseled abs much further down. A part of me wished I could see them.

We walked into the restaurant, and I was immediately struck by the cozy, intimate atmosphere. The bistro was dimly lit, and as we sat down at our table, I noticed that the only illumination came from the flickering candles in the center of the room. Soft music played in the background, and the waves crashing against the shore could be heard through the open windows. Cohen ordered a bottle of red wine, and we ordered our food. Everything was turning out perfectly.

"How are you feeling?" I asked.

Cohen shifted in his chair and winced just a little. Without anesthetic or pain medicine, the wound on his side would ache.

"Not too bad," he replied, even though I knew he was in pain.

A chuckle escaped my lips. "If you need pain medicine, I can write you a prescription."

Cohen smiled and winced again when he started to laugh. "I appreciate that, but I'm going to tough it out. If Dalton can do it, then I can."

The waiter brought us the bottle of wine and filled our glasses, but I sat there stunned. Cohen lifted his glass but then paused when he noticed me staring.

"Did I say something wrong?"

I reached for my wine. "Not at all. I'm just shocked."

His brows furrowed. "About what?"

I took a sip of my wine. "Your mention of Dalton. Are you seriously talking about *Road House?*"

Smirking, Cohen cocked his head to the side. "You've seen the movie?"

I laughed. "Only like a million times. It's one of my favorites."

Cohen chuckled. "It's one of mine, too." He drank more of his wine. "I think we're going to have more in common than you think, Nyla."

"What makes you think I had doubts?" I wondered.

Cohen lifted a shoulder, and his gaze narrowed curiously. "I remember what you said to me the other day at The Beachcomber You said you could spot a city boy from a mile away. That doesn't exactly make me think it was a compliment."

My cheeks burned. "Yeah, I shouldn't have said that. It's just most of the city guys I've dated turned out to be self-absorbed, arrogant jerks who lived off their parent's money. They were also very whiney. But," I added, smiling at him, "you proved you weren't the latter by enduring those stitches today without anesthetic. I'm impressed."

Cohen chuckled and finished off his glass of wine. "Good. I'm glad I could change your perception of me."

I waved a hand at his clothes. "Oh, and there's also how you were dressed today," I confessed. "Even though you were covered in blood, you looked normal in your jeans and T-shirt."

He slipped out of his suit jacket and draped it

over the back of his chair. "And in my suit? What does that make me look like?"

I smiled. "Fancy and rich. I read the article about you in the town paper. You're pretty much royalty in New York."

His smile faded slightly. "I was hoping no one would read that story."

"Why?" I questioned curiously.

He blew out a sigh and looked away. "Because sometimes it's not easy having true relationships when money is involved. I never know if I'm wanted for who I am or because I'm wealthy."

Grinning, I sipped my wine, savoring its complexity and warmth. "If you have to worry about that, I'm afraid you're hanging out with the wrong people."

In my mind, I pictured the smiling faces of my friends in Oak Island—there was Trisha, who had an infectious laugh, and Michelle, who always had something positive to say. Then, there was Everleigh, my best friend and business partner who I loved dearly.

Cohen smiled sadly. "You make it sound so simple."

I shrugged. "That's because it is. But then again, I'm not in your shoes. It's easy for me to say that."

The server arrived with our dinner plates and placed them in front of us; my steak was cooked to perfection with a lightly charred crust, and the broccoli was roasted to bring out its nutty flavor with just enough garlic added to enhance its taste. Cohen thanked the server politely, and I couldn't help but smile at his good manners. He seemed too good to be true, but I had faith in my judgment.

As I cut into my steak, releasing its tantalizing smell, Cohen watched me with a smirk on his face as I enjoyed the first few bites.

"What's so funny?" I asked, taking another heavenly bite of steak.

Cohen shook his head and laughed quietly. "Nothing. I'm not used to seeing women enjoy their food like you do."

"Ah, I see," I said slowly, understanding why he found me amusing; he probably was used to thin-bodied socialites who only picked at their meals. Although I did care about my weight and was active, I loved treating myself now and again, mostly with cakes and cookies. "I'm assuming I'm not like the typical woman you'd take out in New York?" I questioned inquisitively.

Cohen chuckled. "No, but I firmly believe that's been my problem. There was nobody like you there to meet."

My cheeks burned and I smiled. "I highly doubt that. There are tons of amazing women in this world. Just like I know there are good men. I never really thought much about fate, but if you're meant to cross paths with someone, it'll happen."

Cohen's lips pulled back. "So, you're saying we were meant to meet?"

Nodding, I took another bite of steak. "Exactly. And now, the rest is up to us."

He leaned forward, his green eyes sparkling in the candlelight. "I like the sound of that. For starters, do you think you could help me out with something?"

My curiosity was piqued. "With what?"

His eyes dropped to his food, and he grinned. "The other day when I first met you, I asked if you could give me tips on how to become accepted as a local." His focused his gaze to my face, his expression sincere. "I want to fit in here. What do I have to do?"

I reached over and placed a hand over his. "Just be yourself. That's what I did."

His smile faded. "What if it's not enough?"

"It will be," I assured him.

An idea popped into my head, and I squeezed his hand. "What are you doing tomorrow night?"

Cohen cocked his head to the side. "Nothing that I know of. Why?"

"Good," I replied, my excitement growing stronger. "Because I think you need to come with me to The Beachcomber for dinner. I meet all my friends there every Tuesday; it's tradition. It'll give you a chance to befriend them."

He looked down and moved his hand out from under mine so he could take it in both of his. His palm was warm, and I felt a rush of adrenaline course through me.

"So soon? Are you asking me out on a second date?" He raised an eyebrow inquisitively, and my stomach fluttered in response.

"I am. But don't worry, if you don't pass the friends test, then I highly doubt there will be a third," I warned him playfully.

Cohen smiled and gestured to his glass of wine with a nod. "Challenge accepted. What do you think my chances are that they'll like me?"

I shrugged, my grin growing wider. "I think your odds are fair. We'll just have to wait until tomorrow night to find out, won't we?"

Cohen lifted his glass toward me for a toast. "Yes, we will."

5

NYLA

*A*fter we ate, we walked down to the marina and strolled around the docks. It was still early, and I had a feeling Cohen didn't want the date to end. In all honesty, I didn't either. It was the first time I'd enjoyed a man's company since my divorce.

The night breeze was cool against my skin, but Cohen's closeness kept me warm, especially when he took my hand as we strolled. The stars were beautifully bright and vivid in the sky. I could never see them like that in Boston.

"Tell me about your practice," Cohen wondered, his steps slowing as we approached the dock's edge. "What made you want to leave Boston and move here?"

Sighing, I let go of his hand and leaned against the wooden railing so I could face him. "It's funny you should ask that. I never thought I'd make such a drastic move, but everything happened all at once." I looked up at the stars and smiled. "Everleigh, the woman I was with that day you met me, is my best friend. She used to work at Massachusetts General with me." I met his gaze. "But she's from Oak Island. Her father was a doctor; he was the one who owned Seaside Family Practice. He was going to sell it, but then Everleigh decided to move back and take it over. I realized I wanted the same thing when I saw how happy she was here." I shrugged. "Guess you can say I was envious. I wanted happiness, so when Everleigh offered me half of the practice, I jumped at the chance. It was a spontaneous and bold move to leave my life in Boston to come here, but I have zero regrets."

Cohen leaned onto the railing beside me. "What about your family? Do they live in Boston?" he asked, peering over at me.

I nodded. "My parents do. I have aunts, uncles, and cousins everywhere, though. I was never really close to any of them. But my parents are happy for me. They like coming down to visit. I have a feeling they'll move here one day."

Cohen chuckled and turned his attention to the sea. "That'll never happen with mine. Their empire is in New York."

I turned my body around so I could also look out at the ocean. "Are you going to stay in Oak Island, or do you have plans to move back?" I asked, peering over at him.

He shrugged, but there was a slight smile that lifted the corner of his lips as he kept his focus on the water. "Don't know. It all depends on how things go down here." His grin widened, and his green eyes sparkled. "Right now, there are a lot of perks to staying."

My heart skipped a beat. "What made you want to buy out Freddy's Surf Shop? From what I've heard, it doesn't seem like a small business like that would've grabbed your attention all the way up in New York."

Cohen chuckled and looked over at me. "Those are the best businesses to help, Nyla." He waved a hand out at the ocean. "I've read about how beautiful the North Carolina coast is, and when word got to me that Freddy's was suffering, I knew I could help. It's something I wanted to do on my own and not through my father's company. If I happen to settle down roots while I'm here, then so be it. I'm enjoying the coast."

"I'm glad," I said, bumping him with my shoulder. We stared at each other for a few seconds and his gaze drifted down to my lips.

"Want to know what I'm really shocked about?" he murmured, his eyes moving to mine.

"What?" I whispered.

The wind blew a loose strand across my face. He

gently lifted it away, his fingers trailing softly against my cheek. The touch sent shivers down my spine and warmed me inside.

"How can someone like you be single? There have to be men after you all the time."

I couldn't help but grin at his compliment. "I've had a few ask me out since moving here, but I've been focused on building my practice. It wasn't until recently that I decided to try dating again."

Cohen grinned. "Then I guess I got lucky moving here at the right time."

We both laughed softly, but then the smile slowly faded from my face as thoughts of Miles crept in. I knew I couldn't keep my failed marriage hidden from Cohen if we were going to pursue anything serious.

"Nyla? What's wrong?" he asked with concern etched on his face.

The familiar burn threatened behind my eyes, and with a heavy sigh, I turned to look at him fully. "I was married before," I said softly.

His expression shifted from surprise to sympathy. "Really? What happened?"

I laughed but there was no humor to it. "Stupidity," I answered.

Cohen snorted. "Obviously, on his part."

"No," I replied, shaking my head. "It was mine."

Cohen's expression was full of disbelief. "I'm having a hard time believing you. What happened?"

Quickly, I held up a hand. "First off, I didn't cheat. Neither one of us did. My ex was too good of a man to do that to me."

"Then what went wrong?" Cohen wondered; his eyes narrowed curiously.

A heavy sigh escaped my lips. "My ambition is what went wrong. I put all my energy into my job and lost focus on my marriage. My husband wanted to make it work, but I couldn't seem to ever leave the hospital. It was hard to say no when they needed me. Helping people has always been my passion." The familiar sting in my heart came back; it was regret. "The problem," I said, fighting back the burn behind my eyes, "was that I never helped myself, or my husband for that matter. He deserved better than what I gave him."

Cohen cupped my cheeks in his firm grasp. "Hey, don't beat yourself up over the past."

I shrugged. "It's hard not to."

His hands slid from my face. "Do you still keep in touch with him?"

"No," I replied, turning my gaze to the ocean. "It's been over two years since the last time we spoke. My heart hurt too much trying to keep him in my life. I thought a clean break would be best." Cohen wrapped an arm around my shoulder and pulled me into his side. "That's why I buried myself in work. Not long after that, I met Everleigh. She was a lifesaver."

Cohen let out a sigh and guided me down the dock back toward the parking lot. "Look at it this way, if you were still married, you wouldn't be living in Oak Island with your own medical practice. Things *do* happen for a reason. Also," he began, and I could hear the smile in his voice, "if you were still married, you wouldn't be here with me." His voice was low and gentle, like a whisper of a breeze on the ocean water.

I laughed. "That's true."

We stopped at my car and Cohen moved closer, the moonlight outlining his strong jawline. His hands were warm against my cheeks as he leaned in, his gaze never breaking from mine. A thrill ran through me as I waited for him to make the next move. Our breaths mingled as he paused, lips parted slightly.

"I know it's our first date, but I've wanted to kiss you since the second I saw you tonight."

My pulse quickened with anticipation. "Then what's stopping you?" I whispered, feeling the heat rise to my cheeks.

Cohen didn't say anything. Instead, he leaned in and brushed his lips against mine. It was a soft kiss as if he was asking for permission. I didn't hesitate to give in to him. I wrapped my arms around his neck and pulled him closer, deepening the kiss. He tasted like wine and sea salt, and I couldn't get enough of him.

His hands trailed down my back, sending shivers down my spine. Cohen pulled back from the mesmerizing kiss, his thumb caressing my cheek.

"We should probably call it a night," he murmured.

I could only nod in agreement; this was our first date, and I wasn't ready to take things any further than where we had already gone.

"Yes, we should," I said with absolute certainty.

He opened my car door and kissed me again before stepping away. His emerald eyes glimmered in the moonlight as he smiled down at me.

"Have a good day at work tomorrow. I'll see you at The Beachcomber." He glanced down at himself and adjusted his suit jacket self-consciously. "And I promise I'll do everything I can to fit in. No suits, I promise."

That made me laugh. "You do that. But I know that you'll like my friends and vice versa."

He smiled. "I hope so."

He waited for me to hop inside my car and then shut the door. I watched as he got into a shiny silver Bentley that had to be worth a full year of my salary.

Was Cohen too good to be true?

In comparison to Miles, they were like night and day. Miles was a firefighter, handsome in every rugged way possible, not afraid to get his hands dirty, and not rich by any means. We lived comfortably when we were together, and the passion was off the charts.

Cohen was good-looking and polished, a businessman who obviously always gets what he wants. Maybe that was what I needed, someone completely different who wouldn't remind me of the only man I'd ever loved.

6

NYLA

"*T*hank you for letting me use your freezer!" Autumn yelled, her words bouncing off the walls in the garage. "I knew I should've bought a new refrigerator when mine started having issues."

I smiled and shook my head, setting my purse on one of the bar stools. It was almost time for me to meet Cohen and my friends for dinner at The Beachcomber.

"Well, now you have to!" I hollered back, leaning against the kitchen counter.

Autumn scoffed. "I know, it sucks. Good refrigerators are so expensive."

It just so happened that when she'd arrived home from work today, she opened her refrigerator to find out it had died. Luckily, it hadn't been out long because her food was still cold. She took all her refrigerated stuff to her parents' house since they lived closer to her, but they didn't have the freezer space. Since I had an extra freezer in the garage that Jensen had left when he sold me the house, I told her to bring her stuff over.

Autumn appeared in the doorway, and she whistled when she saw me. "Wow. You look great in those tight jeans and cute little top."

The Beachcomber was casual, so I opted for jeans, strappy brown sandals, and a light green, sleeveless top. I smiled at Autumn.

"Thank you. I hope everyone gets along with Cohen tonight. He doesn't act high maintenance, but you can tell he's big money. When they're joking around, Jensen and the guys can be a little crude at times."

Autumn snickered. "If Cohen can't handle that, then he's got issues. We're not stuffy suit people down here."

That was the truth. She crossed her arms over her chest, her expression concerned as if something was on her mind.

"What are you thinking about?" I asked her.

She bit her lip sheepishly and waved me off. "It's none of my business. I mean, I know you're my boss, and we're also friends, but I don't want to overstep. I can get kind of nosy at times."

That made me laugh. "Which means you've

already put your nose in something," I replied, giggling even harder.

Still looking sheepish, she quickly reached into her back pocket and pulled out her phone. "Okay, fine, I have." She moved closer and I watched her type Cohen's name into the search engine. "So, your new boyfriend is kind of a big thing in New York, right?"

I wasn't surprised to see a gazillion pictures and articles pop up about Cohen. Autumn handed me her phone so I could get a better look. She clicked on the pictures and there were so many of Cohen being followed around by the paparazzi; it was as if he was a celebrity. My mouth gaped in shock at all the images.

Autumn bumped me with her elbow. "He's literally treated like royalty, Nyla. The guy is seriously connected. If you wanted to get front-row tickets to any concert, he could get them with a snap of his fingers." She tapped her phone at a picture of Cohen with his arm around the shoulders of a famous actress. "Looks like he probably got the media's attention after dating that one. She's uber popular." Her name was Anne Hatfield and I'd seen several of her movies. She was the epitome of gorgeous with her sleek blonde hair and slender frame. Not to mention she was amazing on screen.

I scrolled through more of the images at ones that were more recent; there were none of him with

Anne. However, there *was* an article about their breakup. It just so happened it was dated over a year ago. At least, it meant I probably wasn't his rebound.

Autumn tapped her phone screen. "If the paparazzi follow him in New York, who's to say they won't come here? You'll be all over the internet if they see you with him."

My stomach dropped. I couldn't imagine being followed by cameras constantly; I loved my privacy. I've read the tabloids and they could be brutal. I could only imagine what they'd say about me. The headline would probably read: *Sexy Bachelor Slums it with Small-Town Doctor who is no Runway Model.*

"Hopefully, they don't know he's here," I said, remembering what Cohen said last night. He wasn't all that happy about the article in the local newspaper. The good thing about that was the newspaper was only in print and not digital. No one would be able to look it up online.

Autumn grabbed her phone and tapped around on it before handing it back to me. "Yeah, they don't know he's here . . . yet," she said, sighing with concern. "But read that article. It was posted just this morning."

I focused on her phone and groaned when I read the headline. *Cohen Sumner has Disappeared from the Social Scene. Where did he go?* It talked about how he was right in the thick of things in New York, going to all the hot parties and clubs, but then, he upped and left. No one knew where he was.

"Great," I grumbled, handing over Autumn's phone. "It's probably a game now on who can find him first."

That wasn't what I wanted to see, but I was glad Autumn told me about the articles. If Cohen attracted that much attention, it was something I needed to know. Autumn slid her cell into her back pocket.

"Are you going to talk to him about it?"

I nodded. "Of course. He never mentioned any of it to me. The paparazzi, nothing."

Could I blame him for not saying anything? No, not really, but it would've been nice to be warned. Autumn patted my shoulder and sighed.

"Good luck with that. I'm sure he didn't want to scare you off. Some women would be all for being in the spotlight, but I know it's not your scene. Cohen probably realized that and didn't want to say anything. He probably thinks he's protecting you."

The thought made me smile, washing away my doubts. "Yeah, maybe so. I can't be mad at him for that."

Autumn chuckled. "Nope. It's actually kind of hot. I like protective men."

So did I.

I glanced over at the microwave clock and grabbed my purse off the bar stool. "All right, I gotta go before I'm late," I said, pushing her toward the door. "I want to talk to Cohen alone before we sit down with the others."

Autumn hurried out to her car, and I went over to my Jeep beside her silver Accord. She waved before getting in and quickly backed out of the driveway. I had ten minutes to get to the restaurant, which was only eight minutes away.

When I got there and pulled into the parking lot, I spotted Everleigh and Jensen's CRV, Michelle and Grady's truck, and Seth and Trisha's blue SUV. Even Cohen's little sports car was at the far corner of the lot. I parked beside him, and my eyes widened in surprise at the sight of him. His dark hair was tousled as if he had just run his hands through it, and he was wearing a plain gray T-shirt and jeans.

He held out his arms and smiled. "What do you think? Do I look like I'll fit in?"

I stepped toward him and returned his smile. "You'll do fine," I said as he embraced me and kissed me gently on the lips.

"I'm ready to go in when you are," he said before stepping back. He noticed me hesitate and furrowed his brows in concern. "Is everything okay?"

I nodded, trying to reassure him even though I could feel my heart hammering nervously against my rib cage. I needed to clarify something but didn't know how to bring up the topic. What was I supposed to say? *Hey, I searched your name online and found you're more famous than I thought.* That sounded ridiculous.

Taking in a deep breath, I let it out slowly. "How popular are you in New York?" I asked, my voice barely above a whisper.

My gaze traveled up and down his figure: the way his emerald eyes sparkled in the dim light of the parking lot, the way his dark hair swayed as he looked away, and the way his jaw muscles tensed as he heard my question.

A few moments passed before Cohen spoke, and his words were heavy with sadness when he did. "What did you see?"

I fidgeted with my fingers nervously. "A million pictures, ones like the paparazzi would usually take." Cohen nodded and looked away, despair radiating off him. "Do they follow you around everywhere?" I questioned.

He closed his eyes for a long moment before opening them again. "I knew this would come up sooner or later. I should've been honest with you from the start. It's just . . ." He paused as if searching for the right words to say.

"It's just what?" I said, my voice soft and understanding.

He turned to me and opened his eyes. "The paparazzi do follow me around in New York and pretty much everywhere I go. My whereabouts have never been a secret . . . until now."

I nodded understandingly. "I figured that. I wouldn't have known any of this if my friend, Autumn, didn't look you up on the internet. I read an article before coming here from some tabloid magazine wondering where you've disappeared to."

Cohen tilted his head back and huffed. "Great."

"Who knows you're in North Carolina?" I asked.

He shook his head and focused on me again. "Only my parents. They know I came here to get away from it all. I'm tired of that kind of life. All I want is to walk down the street and not have someone following me all the time."

He laughed and peered around at our surroundings, but there was no humor to it. It was just us in the parking lot; no paparazzi and no one trying to take his picture. He glanced at it all with longing in his eyes.

"This is heaven to me, Nyla."

The main question I wanted to ask was on the tip of my tongue; I had to know. "What if they find you here, Cohen? What does that mean for us?" *If there was an us*, I thought to myself.

"Does that mean there *is* an us?" He gently gripped my hands in his and pulled me closer to his chest, his expression intense. I didn't know what to say, so I shrugged lightly. It was too soon to put a label on what we were. "I want to get to know you, Nyla," he continued. "I want you to get to know me, the real me. I would love to take you on dates, and then maybe, when you're ready, I would love for the world to know you're mine." His eyes searched mine. "I regret keeping this from you now. We've only known each other a few days, yet I can tell you are not one to shy away from a challenge." His lips curved up in a soft smile as he brushed his thumbs over my cheeks. "We're safe for now, but I'm sure the paparazzi will eventually come looking for me. But if it seems too overwhelming for you, I'll leave and go somewhere else without hesitation."

His words were filled with conviction and left no room for doubt; he was willing to give up his own happiness just so that mine would stay intact. All of a sudden, my mouth felt dry as I looked into his intense gaze.

"You would seriously leave town to keep me out of the press?"

He nodded solemnly. "In a heartbeat. I know how wild it can get."

His touch lingered for a moment before he released me, his palms sliding away from my face.

"It's a good thing I can handle crazy then," I said with a soft laugh. "I was an ER doctor for several years. There was a lot of craziness there."

Cohen blew out a relieved sigh and smiled cautiously at me. "So, you're not giving up on me yet?"

Taking one of his hands in mine, I pulled him through the parking lot toward the restaurant. "Not yet," I replied with a smirk. "You still have to meet my friends. The real test is about to begin."

EVERLEIGH, Jensen, Michelle, Grady, Seth, and Trisha were all sitting at our circular table in the corner when we walked inside the restaurant. It was where we always sat. Everleigh spotted us first and stood, her face glowing as she smiled.

"Hey, you're here!"

Mine and Cohen's talk outside had made us a few minutes late.

"Yes, we are," I laughed, moving over to the two empty seats between her and Trisha.

Jensen, Grady, and Seth all stood, and they shook Cohen's hand while introducing themselves before I could get the chance. It was nice seeing them being friendly with Cohen; there was no doubt in my mind that they wouldn't be. We sat down and Evie came right over to grab Cohen's drink order, which was a beer like the other guys had. She already knew mine would be a Malibu sunset. I'd fallen in love with the fruity drink when she made it for me a few weeks ago.

Everleigh grinned and clasped her hands under her chin. "So, Cohen, how do you like Oak Island?"

Cohen gave her that dashing smile of his that made his cheeks dimple. "I'm enjoying it," he replied, his voice smooth like velvet. His eyes darted to me playfully and he winked. "I've been thinking of taking up surfing."

My mouth dropped and I gasped. "What? You never told me that."

He shrugged and winked again. "I think it could be fun."

Jensen chuckled, garnering Cohen's attention. "If you want to learn to surf, come over to our house," he explained, placing a hand over Everleigh's.

Everleigh nodded in agreement. "Jensen can teach you. It'll be great."

Seth and Grady both chimed in, saying they also wanted to join. Seeing them all welcoming Cohen into the group warmed my heart. Evie returned with a tray with Cohen's beer and my drink on it, but there was also a bottle of champagne and eight flutes, with one of them filled with a bubbly clear liquid that looked like soda; she handed that one to Everleigh.

"All right, let's get this night started," Evie called out. She set the tray down and passed out the flutes.

I took my glass and hooked a glance around the table. "Champagne, huh? Who ordered this and what are we celebrating?"

Evie smirked over at Everleigh, and everyone else tried to hide their smiles as if they already knew what was happening. Evie went around the table and filled our glasses before walking away. Everleigh smiled over at Jensen and he nodded at her. When she focused on me, there were tears in her eyes.

"What is going on?" I asked.

Everleigh beamed and flourished a hand at our filled glasses. "Maybe I should've waited to have the champagne brought out after I got your response. But I'm hoping you'll agree to what Jensen and I want to ask of you." Everleigh placed a hand on her belly and my heart stopped. I knew exactly what she wanted to ask me. "Nyla," Everleigh said, her voice barely above a whisper. I raised my eyebrows in anticipation, and she glanced up at Jensen, her gaze tender before meeting mine again. "Jensen and I want to know if you'd like to be our son's godmother."

My throat tightened and my eyes stung with emotion. I squealed and leaped over in my chair, embracing her.

"Like to? I would *love* to be your son's godmother!"

Tears streamed down my face as she hugged me tightly. Jensen smiled at me from behind Everleigh, his hands held up in defense.

"Granted, we hope nothing happens to us," he said with a chuckle, "but you never know."

Everleigh sat back, wiping the tears from her cheeks as I grasped her hand in mine. "I would do anything for you, Everleigh. There should be no doubt about that."

She nodded solemnly before Jensen lifted his glass of champagne with enthusiastic cheers. We all tossed back our drinks, and Cohen grinned at me over the rim of his glass.

"Question," I announced suddenly, shifting my attention between Jensen and Everleigh. "If I'm the godmother, who do you have in mind for a godfather?"

Everleigh shrugged with an amused smile and gestured toward me. "We trust that whoever you decide to spend the rest of your life with will make a great guardian for our son."

Seth couldn't contain his amusement as he looked over at me. "Hey, maybe you'll find Mr. Right at the Date with a Doctor auction." He winked over at Cohen. "You might have some competition coming up, buddy."

A groan escaped my lips and Cohen looked over at me with his eyebrows raised, clearly amused. "What is this Date with a Doctor auction?"

I nodded over at Everleigh. "It was *her* idea and I only agreed to go along with it if I got to pick the charities the money would go to."

Everleigh waved a hand in the air to get Cohen's attention. "It's for the Spring Fling next month," she explained. "It's a *huge* event. All the vendors usually have a giveaway at their tables to draw people in." She draped an arm over my shoulders. "And what better way to showcase our practice than to show off my beautiful partner."

I rolled my eyes and laughed, hoping my cheeks weren't flaming red with embarrassment. "It's just an ice cream date. Anyone can enter, including kids. It's not exactly a *date*," I emphasized.

Cohen chuckled and leaned in close, his breath warm against my ear. "I have to share you already? It looks like I'll just have to enter and make sure I win."

By the grin playing at the corner of Everleigh's lips, I knew she'd heard what he said. "And how do you plan on winning?" I asked him.

Cohen shrugged, his eyes twinkling with mischief. "Don't you worry about that. I have my ways."

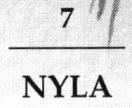

e finished eating and I had a great time; my cheeks hurt from smiling so much. Cohen smiled, laughed, and joked with everyone throughout the night as if he'd been part of the group for years. Trisha shouted her goodbyes, getting into Seth's hulking SUV, and Michelle and Grady waved before they departed in their truck. Everleigh gave me and Cohen one last friendly wave before she and Jensen drove away in her small CRV.

Now we were alone at the far end of the parking lot, surrounded by people strolling the streets, enjoying the ocean air. The faint sound of crashing waves echoed through the starry night sky.

Cohen leaned against his car and playfully pulled me toward him. "I had a good time tonight. Do you think your friends truly liked me?" he asked with a humored grin dancing across his lips.

I chuckled. "Of course they did," I replied warmly, "But I think they're looking forward to watching you try to surf soon." I pushed my lip out in mock concern. "There might even be a bet on how terrible you do."

His laugh filled the air around us and he shook his head lightly. "Let me guess, Seth started that one?"

I nodded with an amused grin on my face. "Yep. He enjoys giving people a hard time—something about two hundred dollars if you fail every time?"

His laughter boomed again as he placed both arms around my waist. "I might have to get Freddy to give me some lessons then. I can't let Seth win."

I smirked teasingly at him. "You will never hear the end of it if he does."

Cohen smiled, his gaze dropping to my lips before meeting my eyes again. "So . . . do you think I can see you again tomorrow night?"

Playfully, I pursed my lips. "That will be our third night in a row."

He shrugged. "Is that so bad? If you want, I can claim a fourth and a fifth. Honestly, I like seeing you every day."

Before I could answer, a gust of wind blew a strand of hair across my eyes, and I swiped it away. But then, a man across the street about to turn a corner caught my attention. My heart stopped and I did a double take, but he was gone before I could get a good look.

Cohen released me from his hold and stepped back, his brows creased with worry. "Nyla, what's wrong?" He asked, clasping my chin.

My chest tightened and it took a second for me to snap back to reality. It couldn't have been *him*. Miles. My ex-husband. The familiar electricity I'd always had when he was around coursed through my body. Swallowing hard, I felt dizzy as a result of how hard my heart was pounding. I stared at the corner where the man had disappeared. He had the same dirty blond hair as Miles, and his body had the same muscular physique that I'd always been attracted to. There were days I couldn't get enough of him. I'd longed to feel that kind of passion with someone again.

"Nyla," Cohen called out, stepping into my line of sight. He scanned the area quickly before focusing on me again. "What did you see?"

"Nothing," I blurted, shaking my head incredulously. "I think I just had a blank moment." Lifting on my toes, I kissed him, trying my best not to let my insecurities spoil the evening. I couldn't exactly tell him that I thought I just saw my ex-husband.

Cohen deepened the kiss, and even though it was nice, all I wanted to do was get in my car and drive through the town. I had to know if it was Miles or if my mind was playing tricks on me. And if it was my mind, I feared what that meant. Cohen searched my eyes, and I forced a smile.

"Are you sure you're okay?" he inquired.

I nodded. "I'm fine, I promise." I gave him another quick kiss. "I'll call you tomorrow after I get off work. We'll figure out our plans then."

Cohen walked over to my Jeep and opened the door for me. "Sounds good. I look forward to it."

I hopped inside and smiled again, desperate to press the gas pedal and get out of the parking lot. Instead of taking a left to go home, I turned right onto downtown's main street. People were walking around everywhere, but I knew I could spot Miles within a crowd. I'd done it before many times; it was as if we were magnets, drawn to each other by some unseeable force. When we were dating, he told me to meet him at one of the bars right by my college campus. As soon as I walked inside, I knew exactly where to look for him. The warmth that would fill me when he was close was undeniable. It didn't take long for me to fall in love with him.

After frantically searching the downtown streets, I had to face the fact that I probably just imagined I'd seen Miles. I thought I was done thinking about him when I decided to move on and start dating again, but it looked like I was wrong.

Once away from the hustle and bustle of downtown and on my way home, I grabbed my phone out of my purse and called Everleigh.

"Hey," she answered. I could hear her car door slam in the background.

"Hey," I replied breathlessly. "Did you just get home?"

"Yep. Jensen and I are going to sit on the back deck for a while. But more importantly, why do you sound like you just ran a marathon?"

A groan escaped my lips. "I think I'm losing my mind, Everleigh."

"Uh-oh, what happened?"

I flung my arms in the air even though she couldn't see me. "Who the hell knows?" I said, turning off the main road onto one of the side streets that led to my house. "Everything was going great, and I was in the moment, but then . . ."

I paused and Everleigh cut in before I could finish. "But then, what? I'm literally sitting on the edge of my rocking chair right now."

I sighed. "I swear I saw Miles. It was uncanny how much this guy looked like him. Granted, I didn't get a good look, but when I did a double take, he was gone." I turned down my street and pulled into the driveway, shutting off the engine. With a heavy groan, I pressed my forehead to the steering wheel. "Why am I seeing him?"

Everleigh's voice turned soft. "Oh, Nyla, I'm sorry. It's probably just that suppressed guilt you keep carrying around. Now that you've started dating again, it's probably just your doubt rearing its ugly head. You need to let it go, or you'll never be happy."

She was right, but it was easier said than done. I was the one who hurt Miles, and I was also the one who ripped out my own heart. I had no one to blame but myself, and I hated it. A part of me feared that I'd never allow myself to be truly happy; I didn't deserve it.

"I know," I said, rubbing the aching spot over my chest. "And believe me, I'm dying to move on. Cohen is an amazing man and an excellent kisser."

Everleigh laughed. "Then concentrate on that. And who knows, you might have been hallucinating. What are the chances of Miles actually being here?"

I snorted. "Slim to none. He never mentioned North Carolina when we were together. Most of the trips we took were out west. Only my parents know I've moved here, and I know they haven't spoken to him."

"And you never post on social media, so we know it couldn't be that way," Everleigh added.

"Exactly," I grumbled, "it's just my mind playing cruel tricks. It's punishing me."

Everleigh huffed in annoyance. "No, it's not. It's

just you being ridiculous. Now concentrate on those amazing kisses you had with Cohen and go from there. I really like him."

That made me smile. "It means a lot that you do."

"When are you going to see him again?"

My cheeks started to warm. "Tomorrow."

Everleigh giggled. "That's three days in a row. Things are getting serious now."

"No, it's not," I said, grabbing my purse and getting out of my Jeep. "I'm taking things slow. Although I am curious to see where all this leads."

Her laugh echoed through the phone. "I can think of a few ways."

I unlocked the front door of my house and snorted. "Not in the first week, crazy ass. The last thing I want to do is rush things."

"Well, if he keeps looking at you the way he was tonight, I don't see how you'll be able to resist him," she added. "The guy is seriously head over heels for you."

With that thought in mind, I walked inside and threw my purse onto the kitchen counter.

"You think?" I wondered.

Everleigh laughed. "Oh, I know. Just don't overthink things when it comes time for you-know-what. You need to enjoy those butterflies and live in the moment."

"Live in the moment," I repeated, the words just

above a whisper. I could feel the excitement of the anticipation bubbling in my chest. "I can do that," I said in all confidence.

That was going to be my new motto: *Live in the moment.*

8

NYLA

ONE MONTH LATER

*I*t was Tuesday night, but Cohen wasn't able to come to the traditional dinner at The Beachcomber like he'd done for the past three weeks. Things have gotten a little hot and steamy with us, but I hadn't *fully* been intimate with him yet. I knew he was ready to take that step, but I wanted a little more time. Was I close to giving in? Yes.

My stomach was stuffed from all the food, so I decided to take a stroll up and down Main Street. I loved looking in the shop windows at all the goodies inside. There were clothing boutiques, jewelry stores, art galleries, and many more shops. I could walk for hours through downtown and never get bored.

My phone started to ring, so I pulled it out of my back pocket and smiled when Cohen's name appeared on the screen.

"Hey, you," I answered, slowing my pace as I weaved around groups of people walking along the sidewalk.

"Hey. What did I miss tonight? Was Seth talking crap about me not being there for surfing tomorrow?"

I couldn't contain my laugh. "Of course," I replied in all honesty. "He thinks you scheduled your New York trip on purpose so you wouldn't have to surf. But don't worry, this week's bet is getting pushed to next week. So, since we're not surfing, I made dinner plans with Autumn for tomorrow. Now if you have to leave again, it will look suspicious."

Cohen chuckled. "I'll be there next week, I promise."

Cohen wasn't as good a surfer as Seth, but he was adamant about not giving up. Seth had already earned close to a thousand dollars in the last month from their bets.

"What are you doing right now?" I asked.

He sighed. "Just got done at the office. I worked late tonight. I'm headed to the restaurant to meet some colleagues for dinner. I wanted to give you a call beforehand. Will you be up a little later tonight?

I want to call you back when there's more time to talk."

"I'll be awake," I promised. "I'll talk to you then."

We said our goodbyes and I slid my phone into my purse, continuing my stroll past the shops to the park at the waterfront. Benches and swings were placed all along the water's edge, and it was the perfect night to enjoy the cool weather.

When I found an open swing, I sat and breathed in the salty sea air. For the past month, I'd spent a couple of hours every evening with Cohen. We took walks on the beach, went out to dinner many times, and I even joined him for some of his surfing lessons with Freddy on top of the weekly ones with Jensen and the guys. Just the other day when I got home from work, a shiny new surfboard was waiting on my front porch.

Cohen wanted me to join him in New York, but I told him I couldn't close the practice for that. In all reality, I could, but I wasn't ready for our relationship to go public. The paparazzi were already looking for him, and I was shocked they hadn't found him these past few weeks. I had no doubt they'd found him in New York, though. Despite myself, I resisted looking him up online to see if any new photos had emerged—maybe it would be better if they stayed focused on him up north rather than coming down here to Oak Island. That was one of the things that held me back from fully committing to Cohen. I didn't know if I'd ever be ready for my life to be publicized like his.

In my eyes, it could only lead to one thing . . . problems.

Ten minutes passed by, and then thirty. It was getting late, so I headed back to the restaurant parking lot to my Jeep. The downtown crowds had died down since it was closing time for a lot of the shops.

When I finally reached the parking lot, I was about to get in my Jeep when I heard a group of guys exit The Beachcomber. With my hand on the handle, I froze as I recognized all three men's voices.

I knew them.

I knew them well even though it had been almost three years since I'd seen them. However, there was only one of those voices that I'd longed to hear. I tried to breathe, but no air would go into my lungs. I turned around to see if my mind was playing tricks on me again.

The second I turned, the world stopped.

I was right.

I wasn't imagining it this time. It was Miles and his two best friends, Noah and Luke. Still frozen, I couldn't take my eyes off Miles. My heart fluttered like it always did when he was near, and I had that undeniable urge to close the distance between us. It took all my strength not to move my feet and go to him to see if he was real.

When my body allowed me to breathe, I sucked in a breath and closed my eyes. When I opened them again, Miles's eyes locked with mine. He stared at me and I stared right back, the memories of our past replaying through my mind. This was why I never wanted to see him again. I knew it would bring up the past and everything I did wrong. The regret was real, and it was debilitating.

Noah and Luke's mouths both gaped and they whispered something to Miles, but Miles never broke his focus on me. He slowly stepped toward me, and all I could hear was my pulse pounding in my ear. My legs felt like lead and there was no moving them. All I could do was stand there while Miles closed the distance.

A small smile lifted the corner of his lips and my eyes burned. I didn't realize how much I'd missed him. His dirty blond hair was a little longer on top, but it still looked the same in that unkempt sort of way that all the women loved. But it was always his crystal blue eyes that managed to make my knees weak. There wasn't anyone alive who had the same eye color as Miles.

"Nyla," he said, his voice so smooth and familiar. He stopped in front of me, his eyes searching mine. "What are you doing here?"

I cleared my throat and released a sigh. "I could ask you the same thing."

His eyes never wavered from mine as he nodded

in Noah and Luke's direction. "Luke's getting married in three weeks," he explained. "We're here for his bachelor weekend, but I'm also here for work."

My heart leaped for joy at the news. Luke was a good guy, and I was happy he'd finally found someone. I used to enjoy hanging out with him when Miles and I were together. The same went for Noah. I glanced at them over Miles's shoulder and waved enthusiastically. Luke and Noah were twins and both firefighters, just like Miles. They looked exactly alike, but Luke's dark hair was shorter and neat, whereas Noah's was a little shaggier.

"Congratulations on the wedding, Luke!" I shouted, grinning happily.

Luke waved back. "Thanks, Ny. It's good to see you!"

It'd been a long time since anyone had called me Ny. Miles used to do it all the time. Miles glanced back at them, and they waved again before getting into a midnight blue Toyota 4Runner.

"So . . . you said bachelor weekend, huh?" I laughed and shook my head. "You picked a low-key place for something like that, didn't you? Oak Island isn't exactly a party town with strip clubs."

Miles chuckled and the sound made me smile. "That's not what we were looking for. We're actually going deep-sea fishing tomorrow morning."

A gasp escaped my lips. "Who's taking you out? Is it McLean Charters?"

Miles raised an eyebrow. "You know them?"

Reaching into my purse, I pulled out one of my business cards and handed it to him. On it was mine and Everleigh's names, along with the name of our medical practice.

"Jensen, the owner of McLean Charters, is my partner's husband." I tapped the card. "Everleigh took over the practice from her father, and she sold me half of it." When Miles's gaze met mine, I felt myself getting lost in it. "I live here now. Oak Island is my home."

Miles sighed in disbelief. "And I'm here, too. What are the odds of that?"

That was a good question. And it was just as I was trying to move on. Silence filled the air as we stared at each other; I couldn't tear my eyes away from him. There were so many questions and things I wanted to know about him. It was crazy to think that Miles and I had once been married. So much had happened since our divorce that now we didn't even know each other. Looking around, I remembered what happened just a few weeks ago when I was in the parking lot with Cohen. I thought I had seen Miles.

"How long have you been here?" I asked.

Miles glanced down at his watch. "Let's see. We arrived about three hours ago." A part of me wished it had been him I'd seen turning that corner, but sadly, it *was* my mind playing tricks on me. When he looked into my face, he peered at me with concern. "Why do you ask?"

"No reason," I said quickly, clearing my throat again. I wasn't about to tell him he was a figment of my imagination when I was standing in almost the exact same spot about to kiss another man. "You said you were here for work. Are you teaching classes like you did before?" I asked.

Miles nodded. "Yep. Starting next week, I'll be teaching Building and Life Safety classes to firefighters around this area."

Not only was he a well-trained firefighter, but he was knowledgeable in so many fields. He used to travel around the country and teach classes when we were married.

"Noah and Luke will be heading back to Massachusetts in three days," he continued, "but I'll be here for another two weeks, and then I'll head back home to Virginia."

A surge of excitement washed through me, and I knew I shouldn't feel that way. But then, the mention of Virginia caught me off guard. "Wait! Did you just say Virginia?" I said, staring at him incredulously. "When did you move there?"

Miles smiled. "You're not the only one who relocated, Nyla. I live in Richmond now. After everything with us, I needed a change of scenery."

My chest tightened and I nodded. "So did I," I agreed. "This place saved me."

I took a deep breath and looked up at the sky. The stars were so bright, twinkling as if they were happy to glitter alongside the moon. Miles stepped closer and I could feel the warmth of his body. My body trembled nervously as I tore my gaze away from the sky to look into his eyes. The intensity behind them was one of the things I loved about him. But it was the last thing I needed to see. What I wanted was to move on, and I couldn't do that with the past staring me right in the face.

"I should probably get back to the guys," he said, his voice dropping to a whisper.

Despite my best intentions to try and start anew, I couldn't help the spark of disappointment that shot through me. "Go," I managed to choke out. "It was great seeing you again. I hope you have a great time while you're here."

Turning on my heel, I took a step toward the driver's side of my Jeep, but Miles grabbed my wrist, halting me. "Nyla, wait."

Swallowing hard, I reluctantly turned around and looked into his eyes again. "I want to see you again," he said hesitantly. "What are you doing tomorrow night? I thought maybe we could catch up after the guys and I get done deep-sea fishing."

The word yes was on the tip of my tongue, but I knew it would only lead to more pain in the end.

Being around him again was intoxicating, but it was also dangerous. I needed to find peace, not torture myself with what once was.

"I'm sorry," I answered, watching his smile fade with my words, "but I have plans tomorrow to grab dinner with one of my nurses at the office."

And just then, my phone beeped with an incoming text. I could see the light on the screen shining in my purse, so I pulled my cell out quickly to see who it was. It just so happened that it was Autumn.

> Autumn: Hey, doc. Wanted to give you a heads up! Can't do dinner tomorrow after work. My new fridge is being delivered!

"Is everything okay?" Miles questioned.

I dropped my phone back into my purse. Was it a sign from the universe? I had to admit it was perfect timing. With Autumn canceling our dinner plans, it meant I was now free tomorrow night.

"That was a text from my nurse, Autumn," I said, wondering if I was about to make the right decision or the worse one possible. "Our dinner plans tomorrow got canceled."

Miles lifted his brows in surprise. "Which means you're free?"

I nodded nervously, not quite ready for the conversation to move forward but unable to deny the hope that was suddenly soaring through me. His grin widened as he stepped closer to me.

"Good. I'll get in touch with you tomorrow afternoon, and we can figure things out from there."

His hand slid from my wrist, leaving behind the warmth of his touch and sending a jolt of electricity up my arm, before turning and walking away. What did I just agree to?

I hopped in my Jeep and Miles glanced over at me once more before getting behind the wheel of the 4Runner and driving off. Once he was out of sight, I frantically pulled my phone from its depths in my purse and pressed the speed dial for Everleigh. My heart pounded uncontrollably as she answered on the second ring.

"Hey," she said. "You're not upset about us canceling the surfing lessons tomorrow, right?"

An exasperated laugh escaped me before I could answer. "Oh, Everleigh, that's the least of my worries right now."

She gasped. "Uh-oh. What happened?"

I leaned my head against the seat. "You will never guess who I just ran into?"

Everleigh giggled. "Let me see . . . Maddox Ledger from the Charlotte Strikers?"

I scoffed. "I wish. That man is hot as sin. But no, not him."

"I have no clue," Everleigh laughed. "Just tell me."

I sucked in a deep breath and let it out slowly. "My ex-husband."

She gasped so loud it hurt my ear. "You can't be serious. What is he doing here? Was it him you saw a few weeks ago?"

I huffed. "He's here for a bachelor weekend, as well as work. And no, it wasn't him I saw. That was all my imagination."

"This is insane, Nyla," Everleigh proclaimed. "And crazy timing, especially since you just started dating again after all this time."

Closing my eyes, I rested my forehead on the steering wheel. "Exactly. I swear my life needs to be made into a soap opera."

"You're damn right about that one. Are you going to see Miles again?"

I tried not to allow myself to feel the excitement swirling through my body, but it was hard. However, there was a bit of guilt plaguing me at the thought of spending time with my ex-husband while in a relationship with someone else.

"I am," I confessed, lifting my head. "We're going to see each other tomorrow after your husband takes him out on a deep-sea fishing adventure."

"What?" she shouted. "This is even crazier. What a small world. Are you going to tell Cohen about spending time with your ex-husband?"

There was no reason to lie to him. I wasn't the type of person to play games.

"Yes," I answered. "I'm going to tell Cohen, and hope he understands. It's not like we're exclusive, Everleigh."

Everleigh chuckled. "That's not because he doesn't want it, my dear friend. Cohen would be all in if you were up for it."

Which was true. I knew Cohen was ready to take our relationship to the next level.

"All Miles and I are going to do is talk . . . that's it," I promised. "I'm sure we won't even see each other again after tomorrow. And then, once he's done with his friends and work, he'll be gone."

"And what if it doesn't go that way?" Everleigh asked. "What if something happens and you find yourself still in love with your ex-husband?"

I felt a twinge in my chest. "Let's just hope it doesn't come to that. If it does, I'm totally screwed."

9

MILES

*L*uke's eyes widened and his jaw dropped as he turned to me. "Dude, how the hell is this even possible? What are the chances of you running into your ex-wife here?"

My chest tightened at the mention of Nyla and I didn't know how to answer Luke's question. There were things I didn't want him or Noah to know.

The whole drive back to our beach rental was a blur. Memories of Nyla flooded my mind. It'd been almost three years since I last saw her, but she wasn't any less gorgeous than before; if anything, she looked even more breathtaking than I remembered. Her wavy red hair and mesmerizing blue eyes were just as I remembered them. And now she had a few more freckles on her face from all the sun.

The salty ocean air mingled with my thoughts as we pulled up to the house. With shaking hands, I parked in the driveway, the sand crunching under the wheels of the car.

"Are you okay, brother?" Luke asked, placing a hand on my shoulder.

I shrugged him off and took a deep breath, trying to push away the overwhelming emotions that consumed me. Was I okay? No, I wasn't. Seeing Nyla again only accentuated how much I missed her. I stumbled out of the car and made my way toward the house, Luke and Noah following closely behind.

The beach rental was cozy, with a small living room and a kitchenette. I walked straight to the fridge, pulled out a beer, and popped the top off. Luke watched me carefully, clearly concerned.

"Talk to me, man. What's going on?"

I took a deep swig of the beer, feeling the cold liquid slide down my throat. "I don't know, Luke. Seeing Nyla again brought back all these feelings I thought I had buried long ago."

Luke nodded, understanding. "Yeah, I get it. But you know she's your ex for a reason, right?"

I knew he was right, but it wasn't for the same reasons most people divorced over. Nyla and I had a passionate relationship full of highs and lows. In the end, we just couldn't make it work. I wanted so much more of her, more than she could give. But part of me still wondered if things could have been different if we had tried harder. Nyla was all about her career, and I could only do so much fighting before it pushed her away. All I was ever guilty of was loving her too much. Nyla was just never around to see it. That was why I initiated the divorce, hoping it would make her want to work things out.

I let out a sigh and took another swig of beer. "I know, Luke. But being around her again just brings back all these memories. Memories of what could have been."

Noah chimed in, "You know, maybe this is your second chance."

I rolled my eyes, "Noah, you've been watching too many rom-coms. There are no second chances in real life."

But deep down, a part of me wanted to believe him. Maybe it wasn't too late for Nyla and me.

"Are you going to see her again?" Luke asked.

I looked over at him and nodded. "Tomorrow after our fishing trip."

He laughed and shook his head. "I should've known. Who knows, maybe my brother's right. This could be your second chance. I mean, hell, you haven't been happy with anyone since Nyla. Maybe these past two years have changed her. If she's a small-town doctor now, I doubt she'll be working those seventy hours she was when you two were together."

Nyla had worked so much that I barely recognized her at times; it was as if her career had sucked the life out of her. She didn't look like that now; she looked happy and content.

Was it possible for Nyla and me to get a second chance? Maybe it was me having a foolish heart or the inability to fully let go, but I had to give it a shot.

I fell in love with Nyla many years ago, and after our divorce, I tried to convince myself that I could get over her. But as the years went by, I still longed for her touch, her laugh, and the way she used to look at me with those piercing blue eyes. Now she was within my grasp once more, and I couldn't let her go without seeing what we could be again.

The moment I saw Miles, it was as if the world finally made sense. Seeing him made me feel like I was back in Boston—when he and I were married and crazy in love. I couldn't deny he still affected me, but he wasn't the only one vying for my attention. I had Cohen now, a man who stole my breath with just a glance, and I cared about him. Our relationship was new and exciting, with the potential to be something more. But how could I explain this to him? How could I tell Cohen that my ex was in town and wanted to spend time with me?

The thought made me feel lightheaded, as if all the air had been sucked from the room. My shirt clung to my body, damp with sweat, and my hands shook uncontrollably as I unlocked the door and stepped into my home.

I dreaded the conversations ahead and the

awkwardness of explaining everything to Miles and Cohen.

It was getting late, so I took a quick shower and put on my pajamas while waiting for Cohen to call. I grabbed a bottle of wine from the refrigerator and didn't even bother pouring some into a glass; I drank straight from the bottle. With the conversation I was about to have, I needed all the help I could get.

After a few minutes, my brain began to feel fuzzy and I welcomed it. I wandered out to the back deck, where I sat in an Adirondack chair and watched as the twinkling lights from the houses across the sound shimmered like diamonds on the sea; it was magical. This place was so different from my apartment in Boston. Instead of hearing horns blaring and the hustle and bustle of people walking down the street, I traded it for the sound of seagulls cawing in the sky and the crashing of waves. I was never going to go back to city life again.

As I sat there and let my mind drift off, my phone suddenly rang, startling me. It was Cohen, and my heart raced as I answered.

"Hey," I said, trying to sound nonchalant.

"Hey," he replied. "I'm sorry I'm calling so late. I didn't want a whole night to go by without really getting to talk to you."

Grabbing the bottle of wine, I took a quick swig. "You're a busy man, Cohen. I understand that. I don't expect you to call me all the time."

The line went silent, and I held my breath. Did I say something wrong? But then the sound of his deep voice came back over the line.

"Is it bad that I *want* you to expect that? I'm starting to fall for you, Nyla, and I always think about you. I'm not ashamed to admit that you've completely mesmerized me. I want you to know I'm fully invested in seeing where this goes."

Of all the nights for him to declare that, why did it have to be now? I looked over at my bottle of wine, wishing I could down it all.

"That means a lot to me, Cohen," I murmured. "It's been a long time since I've found someone who wasn't a complete arrogant douche who only cared about himself."

His laugh echoed through the phone. "I'm pretty sure you thought I was going to be like that the first day we met."

I couldn't help but giggle. "You're absolutely right. I admit I was wrong."

We both laughed together, but then I knew I had to say something about Miles.

"How was dinner tonight with everyone?" he asked.

"Great," I answered. "I was supposed to grab food with Autumn tomorrow after work, but her refrigerator is finally being delivered after waiting a month."

Cohen scoffed. "It's about damn time. I hate she had to wait that long."

"True, but she was very specific about what she wanted," I reminded him. "The store clerk warned her it was on back order."

After waiting a week, Autumn regretted her decision but stuck through it. Silence filled the air, and I tried to think of a way to bring up Miles, but nothing came to mind.

"Are you okay, Nyla?" Cohen asked. "You're usually more talkative than this."

Honesty. It was the only solution.

"That's because I have something to tell you," I admitted nervously.

Cohen sighed. "Why do I not like the sound of that?"

"Probably because you're not going to like it." I took a deep breath and released it slowly. "I ran into my ex-husband today. It was very random, and I had no clue he was in Oak Island. The last time I saw him was over two years ago."

The line went silent again. He was probably letting the information process.

"Is he there to see you?" he asked, his voice guarded.

"No," I blurted, hoping it would ease the tension. "He's here with some friends, but he's also here for work. He didn't even know I lived here."

Cohen blew out a frustrated breath. "When is he leaving?"

I bit my lip. "Not for another couple of weeks."

I could hear his grumble, even though it sounded as if he tried to mute it. "Do you still care about him, Nyla?"

My chest tightened. "I will always care about him, Cohen. Our relationship ended because of me. My ex is a good man, and *I* was the one who hurt *him*, not the other way around."

"So, what happens now?" he asked.

I peered out at the water, wishing some kind of wisdom would come to me, but there was nothing. "He asked if he could see me tomorrow." I squeezed my eyes shut, waiting for his response.

"And what did you say?"

I opened my eyes and leaned back in my chair. "I said yes. And before you start thinking the worst, just hear what I have to say." A shaky breath escaped my lips. "I never got closure after the divorce. When things ended, I thought it was best to go our separate ways and cut ties completely. The guilt weighed heavy on my chest this entire time. I want to make sure he's happy. If he is, I truly believe I can fully move on."

"Is that what's holding you back from me?" he questioned.

"Yes," I answered honestly. It was what held me back from many things.

Cohen sighed again. "Then do what you need to do, Nyla. I care about you, and I want us to work." It felt as if the weight on my chest had lightened, and I could breathe.

"Thank you, Cohen. This is going to help me, I promise."

He groaned. "I just wish I was there. Friday can't get here soon enough."

I laughed. "What exactly do you think is going to happen?"

Cohen scoffed. "Nyla, you're a beautiful, smart woman, and amazing as hell. Any man worth a damn would be able to see that. Something tells me your ex will be reminded of what he lost. And if that happens, I don't see him leaving so easily."

I shook my head even though he couldn't see me. "It won't be like that. He's not going to change his whole life around to follow me to Oak Island. Our relationship didn't work, end of story."

"You'd be surprised what a man would do for the woman he wants."

His words sent trembles through my body. It was sexy to have a man fight for the woman he wanted, but that wasn't the case with Miles. We were going to talk, and then he'd go his own way. In two weeks, he'd be back in Virginia.

"Miles doesn't want me," I assured him. "When you get back, you and I will pick up where we left off. Besides," I said, sounding more cheerful, "the

Spring Fling auction is Saturday. You said you were going to win our date."

Cohen chuckled. "You're right." But then the humor was gone. "Will your ex be there?"

A nervous laugh escaped my lips. "I have no clue," I replied, honestly not knowing. "If he does make an appearance at the Spring Fling, I highly doubt he'd enter the auction. He's not going to want an ice cream date with me."

"Good," Cohen said, "I refuse to let another man win."

However, there was a part of me that wished Miles did enter. But the last thing I needed was for Cohen and Miles to butt heads. The best scenario was for Miles and me to get our closure, and for him to return to Virginia so I could move on.

Yes, that was what needed to happen.

Would it? Guess we'd find out.

"*I* can't believe you're meeting your ex-husband tonight," Autumn exclaimed, her eyes widening with excitement.

I winced and stepped inside my office, draping my lab coat around the back of my chair as I moved to sit down.

"I never should've told you," I said, trying not to sound as panicked as I felt. "It's not like that."

Autumn gave me a knowing smirk as she crossed her arms over her chest and took a few steps closer to my desk. "I would've found out eventually. This town is too small for secrets like that—especially when it involves one of our town doctors."

"Great," I grumbled, reaching for my cell.

"Plus," she said, coming over to stand in front of my desk, "if you go out in public with Miles, people will see you and ask questions. The only way to avoid it is to go to another city where no one knows you."

I shook my head and waved her off so she'd think it wasn't a big deal when actually it was. I didn't want people talking about my love life; everyone knew I was seeing Cohen. He was known as the savior of the town ever since he rescued Freddy's Surf Shop from going under.

"I'll think of something." I ended up saying.

I checked my phone, but there were no messages from Miles. I knew he'd spent the day on Jensen's boat with his friends. However, there were a few messages from Cohen saying he hoped I was having a good day and that he couldn't wait to get home. I slid my phone into my purse.

"All right, let's get out of here. Has Gina locked up the front?"

Autumn nodded. "Yep. We're all set to go. She wanted me to tell you to have fun tonight."

Rolling my eyes, I slung my purse over my shoulder. "You two are going to drive me insane."

Autumn snickered and disappeared down the hall to the break room. "You love us, though," she shouted. "I'm just ready to get my new refrigerator!"

"I bet," I hollered back.

After shutting off my office lights, I walked down the hall toward the back door with Autumn right behind me. When I opened the door to let Autumn out, my mouth dropped open when I noticed our cars weren't the only ones in the parking lot. Parked beside mine was the midnight blue 4Runner Miles had driven off in last night. He was in the front seat and opened the door when he saw us. So many emotions whirled inside of me at the sight of him. There was no denying the regret that plagued me, but something else overshadowed that . . . joy. It brought me comfort to see him.

What did that mean? I had no clue.

Autumn grabbed my arm, her excitement palpable. "Is that your ex-husband?"

Miles waved and smiled at us, his face and arms already tanned from spending the day out in the sun. Even his dirty blond hair appeared brighter. Maybe it was the yellow T-shirt he was wearing that made him appear as if he was glowing in the sunlight.

I smiled at Miles but spoke through my teeth to Autumn. "It is," I answered her. "You better be on your best behavior."

Autumn snorted and winked at me. "Aren't I always?" We walked down the stairs from back porch and she bumped me with her elbow. "He is so much hotter than Cohen," she whispered.

Miles did have that rugged air about him that Cohen didn't. Again, they were two totally different men. Autumn picked up her pace so she could get to Miles first.

She held out her hand and smiled. "Hi, Miles. I'm

Autumn," she said, introducing herself. "I work for Dr. Clark."

Miles grinned wider and shook her hand. "It's nice to meet you, Autumn."

Autumn beamed over at me quickly before focusing back on him. "Same." She let his hand go and walked backward toward her car. "I should probably get going. You two have a good night." She waved and got in her car, winking at me before pulling away.

"She seems like she'd be fun to work with," Miles said, laughing.

I snorted in response. "You have no idea. But I wouldn't trade her in for anyone else."

His smile as he gazed past me toward my office warmed my heart. "This place is all you, Nyla. It suits you."

"It does," I agreed, taking in the bright green building that I'd grown to love so much.

"Was it a slow day?" he asked, his gaze slowly meeting mine again.

I shrugged noncommittally. "Yes and no. Things don't usually get too crazy here. I keep waiting for someone to come in with a shark bite, but it hasn't happened yet. The only serious case I had today was a teenage boy who got stung by a dozen bees. His parents rushed him in just as his throat started to close up. Once I gave him the EpiPen, he could breathe again."

I could still feel the rush of adrenaline from that moment. The look of terror on the parents' faces was something I would never forget. I didn't have children, but I could only imagine how scared the parents were.

Miles blew out a relieved sigh. "Thank God, the boy's okay."

I nodded. "Trust me. I was praying the entire time." I waved a hand in the air. "But enough about that. How did it go fishing today? Did you and the guys have a good time? Did you catch anything?"

Miles nodded excitedly, his expression filled with enthusiasm. "We had a great time. Jensen was an amazing boat captain. We caught a ton of fish." He patted a hand on the hood of his car. "It just so happens that I packed some of that fish up in a cooler. I wasn't sure if you wanted me to bring it to your place, or you come to where I'm staying." He shrugged. "Or we can do something else. I didn't know if you wanted to talk around Noah and Luke, or if you had other plans in mind."

Mine and Autumn's previous conversation echoed in my head. It was a small town and if the locals saw me with Miles, it would bring up questions I didn't want to answer. But if I invited Miles back to my house, we would be alone and away from prying eyes. The only problem with that was Cohen; he wouldn't like it.

He was just going to have to trust me. It was only

for one evening, and I was probably never going to see Miles again.

"Let's go to my house," I suggested, hoping the nerves in my stomach would calm down. "We can cook some of the fish for dinner." My stomach growled. "I'm starving."

Miles beamed. "Perfect. I'll follow you there."

I hopped in my Jeep, and he followed me to my house. I was so nervous for him to see it. There was a time many years ago when he mentioned he wanted to retire to a beach house. What he wanted was exactly what I got. I didn't plan for it to happen like that; it just did. It was another reason why it was hard to forget about Miles. Every time I was at the house, it reminded me of what he wanted for our future, a future I never thought to envision.

I pulled into the driveway and watched Miles's face in the rearview mirror. His eyes widened, and he opened his door slowly. When I got out, he looked at me, his face full of shock.

"Do you know what this place reminds me of?"

I nodded. "I know . . . your retirement home."

He chuckled. "Exactly."

He turned to me and sighed. "I'm happy for you, Nyla. Honestly, I'm a little jealous right now."

He walked over to the side of the house where I knew he'd be able to see my dock and the boat. The second his mouth dropped, I knew that was what he saw.

"You have a boat?" he called out, mouth gaping in shock.

I laughed and shook my head. "It's Jensen's. This house was his, but he sold it to me when he and Everleigh decided to move into her place."

Miles walked back over to me. "Yeah, he told me that."

I narrowed my gaze. "What else did he tell you?"

Miles shrugged and leaned against his car. "Not much. He told me how Everleigh asked you to be her partner at Seaside and how everyone in town loves you."

I waved him off. "Please. That's not true."

And just then, a familiar voice shouted from across the road. "Good evening, Dr. Clark!"

I turned to see George waving at me from his front porch. With a warm smile, I waved and hollered back.

"Good evening, George! Are you and Rose doing okay?"

He pointed toward the door of his house and continued to rock in his rocking chair. "We're doing great. My bride is in the kitchen making lemon bars for tonight. She wanted to try something different from the cookies. I'll bring you some over in the morning."

I clutched my stomach so he'd know I was ready for them. "Can't wait! I'm looking forward to them."

I turned back to Miles and he lifted his brows. "I

rest my case. The people here love you. There's no denying that."

I tilted my head in George's direction. "I'm lucky that I have great neighbors. George and Rose are like grandparents to me. Rose made some lemon cookies the other week that I demolished."

Miles laughed. "And now she's making you lemon bars. We didn't have people like that in Boston."

I shook my head. "No, we didn't. Oak Island is seriously another world entirely. I can't imagine being anywhere else."

A sad expression crossed his face, but he turned and opened his car door, pulling out the small blue and white cooler.

"How about you show me to the grill, and I'll cook us some dinner."

I grabbed my purse and started for the door. "I can do that. I'll work on our sides."

Miles followed me inside and I showed him around the house before getting started on cooking in the kitchen. He prepped the fish and got the grill going while I put our baked potatoes in the oven and washed the lettuce for our salads.

Once that was done, I watched Miles as he stood outside by the grill. There was something on his mind; I could see it in his eyes. I may have been an absentee wife when my career started, but there was a time when I knew him better than anyone; there was a time when our lives were perfect. I'd give anything to feel that way again.

My phone beeped and I grabbed it off the kitchen counter to see a text from Cohen.

> Cohen: Do you mind if I call you later tonight?

> Me: That works perfect. I'll talk to you then.

There was no asking what my plans were for the evening or how everything was going with my ex, but I had a feeling he didn't exactly want to know. Maybe that was a good thing.

12

MILES

*W*hen I planned the trip to Oak Island, I never expected things to hit me the way they did. I'd known for three months that Nyla had moved to the North Carolina coast. And it took me those three months to make the decision to find her. I wanted to gauge her reaction to me before I told her the truth that I purposefully scheduled work and the bachelor party for Luke in Oak Island so that I could find a way to see her.

The guys didn't know; it was my secret.

I didn't want them to tell me I was an idiot for going after Nyla after everything that happened. For the past while, I thought I could date other women and forget about her, but nothing worked. Seeing Nyla now, I was sure I'd made the right choice. She still cared about me. I saw it in her eyes the second they locked with mine.

I took a deep breath and let it out slowly as I watched a small boat putter down the channel. The sun was about to set, casting an orange and purplish glow in the sky. There were so many things I wanted to ask Nyla, things that could change everything. I knew she was seeing someone, only I didn't know how serious it was.

While on the boat with Jensen, I asked him if she was dating anyone, and he hesitated. I could only assume that meant she was. However, I wanted to believe it wasn't serious given she invited me over tonight.

Or it could be the total opposite and worse than I could've imagined.

If she and the other guy were close, it could mean he didn't consider me a threat, especially if he knew she was with me right now.

The back door opened, and I turned to see Nyla stick her head out. She smiled and nodded inside.

"The baked potatoes are done, and I made our salads." Her gaze caught the sunset off in the distance and her mouth dropped. "Oh, never mind, I think we need to eat out here." She focused back on me and lifted her brows. "Does that sound good to you?"

I nodded. "Perfect. The fish is almost done."

Nyla disappeared inside and came out a few seconds later carrying a tray with two plates, our baked potatoes, salads, and a pitcher of tea.

"Let me guess," I said, opening the grill and setting our perfectly cooked red drum on the small pan off to the side. "Is that unsweetened raspberry tea you got there?"

I put the plate of fish in the middle of the table and watched Nyla pour me a glass before sitting across from me. Raspberry tea was all she used to drink when we were together.

Nyla laughed and shook her head. "Actually, it's not. I know you hated the stuff. When I moved here, I decided to try something new." She flourished a hand toward the pitcher of tea. "It's blueberry. If you don't like it, I'll get you something else."

I'd always tried to get her to make new flavors, but she was always too tired from work to even consider it. That woman wasn't the same one sitting before me.

Picking up the glass with one hand, I took a sip while Nyla watched my reaction expectantly.

"It's pretty good," I confessed truthfully.

She clapped her hands and laughed. "I'm glad you like it. I remember you asking me to try new flavors and I never did." Her smile faded slightly as she lifted her glass. "I was seriously missing out and didn't even know it."

I shrugged off her reply, not wanting to throw the past in her face. That time was over. If I wanted to accomplish what I came here to do, there was no room for that.

Taking my fork, I speared a piece of fish from the pan on the table and placed it next to my baked potato on the plate.

"Yeah, but you're enjoying everything now."

Nyla filled up her plate with fish and nodded, her smile sad. "I'm trying to."

We spent the next few minutes eating our food in silence. It was nice just being able to spend time with her, but I could tell she had a lot weighing on her mind. After eating, Nyla dropped her fork on her plate, the sound echoing all around us.

"Okay, I just want to come out and say this," she blurted.

There was nothing but determination on her face. She reached over and grabbed my hand; her skin was so soft I didn't want her to let go.

"I just want to say how sorry I am for how things ended. I haven't been able to get closure. All I wanted back then was never to see you again. I thought that if I didn't, I wouldn't be reminded of how badly I screwed up. I thought the guilt and regret would go away."

I squeezed her hand. "And did it?"

Tears filled her eyes. "No. That's why I'm glad you're here. I need to hear it from your lips that you forgive me. I don't think I can move on without it."

Those weren't exactly the words I wanted to hear from her.

"Is that what you want?" I asked. "To move on?"

She rubbed a hand over her chest. "I don't think I can handle the guilt anymore, Miles. It's the only thing that keeps me from being fully happy." She shrugged. "Well, that, and hoping that you've been able to find happiness after everything I put you through." I shook my head, but she held up a hand. "Are you happy? And I need you to be completely honest with me."

The truth was not what she needed to hear now; it wasn't the right time.

"I am," I lied. "You don't need to worry about me."

There was a hint of sadness on her face. "So, you've moved on?"

I nodded, but it wasn't in the way that I knew she was asking.

"I'm happy, Nyla," I said, placing my other hand on our clasped ones. "I don't want to be the cause of you being miserable. What happened in our past changed us . . . for the better. You are where you're supposed to be. And I am, too."

With her.

Her eyes looked deep into mine as she squeezed my hand and let go.

"It really is good to see you."

"Same," I murmured. "And it would be nice if we could keep in touch. I would rather have you in my life than not at all."

She looked down at the remnants of her leftover food and poked her fork around the inside of her potato. I had a feeling the mention of her new boyfriend was about to come up. That was what I wanted; I wanted to know who he was in her life.

"Miles," she whispered, letting out a strangled breath. She paused and stared at me, but I was the one who spoke.

"Let me guess . . . you're seeing someone, and it'll cause problems," I said.

Her eyes widened and that was my answer. "I was going to tell you," she started, then sighed. "But my mind has been all over the place with seeing you."

"Seeing me?" I questioned. "What does that mean?"

Panic flashed across her face and she stood, her attention focusing on the dirty plates. "I need to clean up. It's getting late."

She piled the plates all together in her arms and rushed inside. I grabbed the rest of the dishes, along with the pitcher of tea, and went in to see her washing everything haphazardly. Carefully, I placed everything on the kitchen counter and stood there, wishing I could pull her into my arms as I'd done many times before. There were so many different ways tonight could go, but I had to hope for the best. If Nyla wanted closure, it was time to put everything on the line.

Before I could speak, Nyla's voice cut through the silence, her back to me as she stood by the sink, her shoulders tense and her hands gripping the countertop.

"Jensen said something, didn't he?"

"Not exactly," I replied. "When I asked if you were with someone, I could sense he didn't want to tell me, so I let it go." I took a step toward her. "How long have you been with this guy?"

She glanced at me over her shoulder. "Not long. Just about a month."

A lot could happen in a month. Nyla and I were only together for three weeks before I told her I loved her.

"Do you love him?" I asked, stepping closer.

Slowly, she turned to face me, confusion playing across her features. "I care about him, Miles. I was being truthful when I said I needed closure with you. I haven't been able to move on without it. It's hard to love someone new when . . ."

She cut off her words and bit her lip, clearly not wanting to continue her sentence. My pulse pounded in my ears as I took another step toward her. I wanted to hear the rest.

"Tell me, Nyla," I said, stepping up to her. "I want you to finish that sentence."

She shook her head and looked away. "It'll only make things more difficult."

"Why? Because you still have feelings for me?"

I wanted to know that I wasn't the only one

holding onto what we had. Her shoulders fell and she closed her eyes, her voice just above a whisper.

"I never stopped loving you, Miles. That's the problem."

I cupped her cheeks and lifted her face, waiting for her to open her eyes. When she did, I pressed my lips to hers. As we kissed, all the emotions that had been bottled up inside me for so long came to the surface. I felt the warmth of her lips, the softness of her skin, and the tenderness of her touch. It was as if time had stopped, and we were back to that moment when we first fell in love.

We pulled away, both gasping for breath. Her eyes were filled with tears as she looked at me, and I knew that what we had wasn't over.

"I'm sorry," she whispered. "I shouldn't have let that happen." She moved away from me and ran her hands through her hair. "What am I going to do?"

"I want you to choose *me*, Nyla," I said, closing the distance again. I grabbed her hands and pulled her to me. "You still love me, and I love you. I didn't lie when I told you I was happy." I placed her hands on my heart. "I'm happy because I'm *here* . . . with you."

She shook her head and jerked her hands out of my grasp. "None of this would've happened if you didn't just accidentally show up. You didn't even know I was here. It's not like you came looking for me."

That was where she was wrong. I stood there and smiled, loving how her cheeks always turned red when flustered.

"Come on, Nyla," I said, smirking. "Do you honestly think out of all the places in the world to go deep-sea fishing, it's coincidence that I chose this exact spot?"

She stared at me for a few moments before surprise and suspicion hit her like a wave. "Are you saying . . ." Her mouth gaped and she held up a hand. "You knew I was here?"

I nodded, my grin growing wider. "For three months."

Exasperated, she shook her head. "How?"

Reaching into my pocket, I pulled out my phone and searched her name, showing her everything that popped up.

"It's not hard to look someone up, Nyla. Imagine my surprise when I saw you connected to Seaside Family Practice as one of the doctors. After that, I built up the courage to make my move. I convinced Luke this was the perfect place for his bachelor weekend."

Nyla's mouth gaped, but then her eyes blazed with that fiery temper that matched her red hair. She pushed against my chest and huffed.

"Three months? Three months!" Her arms flung in the air. "If you'd just gotten here a month earlier, I wouldn't be in this predicament. Now what am I supposed to do?"

I couldn't blame her for moving on with another man; I should've come sooner. It was easy to tell her to choose me and let the other guy go, and I wasn't about to give her an ultimatum. But I sure as hell wasn't going to make it easy on her.

Nyla was clearly confused, and I knew she'd reached her limit; a lot had been revealed tonight. I wanted to kiss her again, to feel her in my arms, but instead, I grabbed my car keys off the kitchen counter. Nyla had much to consider, and I knew she wouldn't find a solution tonight.

She glanced down at the keys in my hand and huffed. "Are you seriously leaving after dumping all those truth bombs on me?" Nyla always had a way of making me laugh.

"I think it's for the best. You always liked having your space when someone pissed you off."

Her expression softened. "I'm not mad at you, Miles." There was a hint of sadness in her voice but also understanding. "I just know that things are about to become complicated. Yes, I love you, and you were my husband for a time, but I also care about someone else. He's good to me. The last thing I want to do is hurt either of you."

My heart raced as I looked into her eyes, searching for the truth. "Can you see yourself with that other guy for the rest of your life? Do you have the same fire, the same passion when he touches you?"

My hands brushed against her face and our skin ignited. She felt it too—the electricity that sparked between us and refused to be ignored.

"Does it feel like that when he touches you?"

Her gaze dropped to the ground; the answer was written all over her expression.

No.

I wanted to pull her in and kiss her until she forgot about anyone else, but instead, I stepped away, lifting a hand to caress her cheek one last time.

"You might want to ask yourself why that is," I said softly before turning and walking to the door. I stopped and touched the handle, smirking at her over my shoulder. "Oh, and one more thing."

Nyla pursed her lips and crossed her arms over her chest. "What else is there? I'm already going to have a horrible night telling a certain someone that I kissed my ex-husband tonight."

My brows shot up. "You're going to tell him?"

She huffed out an incredulous breath. "How can I not? He trusted me to spend this evening with you and even warned me that something like this would happen. I'm going to tell him the truth."

I shrugged. "Maybe it's a good thing you tell him. Maybe he'll realize it's not meant to be."

She bit her lip. "He's not the type of guy to give up so easily. If anything, it's going to make things really awkward. He'll try harder to make me choose him."

That was not what I wanted to hear. One thing was for sure—this enigmatic "certain someone" didn't have the same shared history Nyla and I did.

I opened the door and smiled, but my heart was in my throat. "I'm not giving up, Nyla," I said, putting as much emotion into each word as possible. "I came here for a reason: to get you back. Am I a little too late? Yeah, maybe, but that's why I'm going to work extra hard. If you decide I'm not the one, I'll leave and let you move on."

Nyla stood there with her arms still crossed, but I could see the desperation on her face. Whoever this other guy was, I know she didn't love him. She was afraid, and that fear was keeping her from me. I just had to make her see that we needed our second chance and what happened in the past shouldn't scare her anymore.

I walked out to my car and glanced back at the door where Nyla stood, her eyes full of turmoil. I didn't want to make things difficult for her, but being without her for was not what I wanted.

When I asked for the divorce, I hoped it would make Nyla realize what she was throwing away. It hurt when she didn't try to work things out. I had no choice but to see the divorce through. If I'd only tried harder to make her see that our marriage could've worked, maybe we'd still be together.

Nyla stepped out of the doorway. "How is this going to work, Miles? I'm stuck between a man from my past who I loved more than anything, and another one who I could potentially see a future with. I don't know what to do."

A pang of jealousy sparked in my gut. I didn't like her seeing a future with the other guy, but it was something I was going to have to deal with.

"You'll figure it out, Nyla. You just have to trust yourself," was all I could say.

Her lips pulled back in a slow smile. "That's easier said than done."

I shrugged. "I have faith in you. I always have."

Nyla raised her brows inquisitively. "So, what exactly is next on your game plan? You come here to profess your love and now what?"

I met her gaze head on. "Oh, I don't know," I said, my lips spreading into a smirk. "Somebody told me about this Date with a Doctor auction at the Spring Fling this Saturday."

Nyla's mouth dropped. "Please tell me you're not going to it." I hopped in my car and she raced over, blocking me from shutting my door. "Miles, seriously? Are you going to enter?"

I tapped her chin playfully. "I think an ice cream date with you sounds fun."

She rolled her eyes, but the corners of her lips tugged up slightly, revealing that she was secretly happy about it, too.

"You're not the only one, you know."

I winked at her. "Didn't think I would be. Maybe I'll be lucky and win."

Nyla laughed softly and it was exactly what I needed to hear. "Maybe you will." She stepped back. "Looks like I'll be seeing you later."

I shut my door and rolled down my window. "Yes, you will."

And with those final words, I left.

13

NYLA

*M*y heart was beating so hard against my sternum that it felt like I would pass out. I hurried inside and tried to catch my breath, only nothing worked. Even the cool breeze of the fan spinning overhead did nothing to ease the fire burning within me.

Earlier in the day, I'd had a million different scenarios run through my mind on how tonight was going to go with Miles. The last thing I ever expected was for it to end the way it did.

Was seeing Miles again and working things out something I'd dreamed about for a long time? Yes. But now it wasn't so simple. I had Cohen.

My phone was on the coffee table, so I rushed into the living room and snatched it up. Thankfully, Cohen hadn't called yet. I wasn't ready to tell him about everything that had happened.

My heart started to race again as I called Everleigh. If anyone had good advice, it was her; I sure as hell didn't know what to do. After two rings, her cheerful voice came through the line.

"Hey," she said. "I was hoping you'd call me tonight. How did it go with Miles?"

I laughed but there was no humor to it. "Let's just say it wasn't what I expected. I'm in a crap ton of trouble and I don't know what to do." I glanced over at the kitchen clock; it was already close to 9:30 p.m. "I know it's late, but I could really use your advice. Plus, I need to get out of the house."

"Of course," Everleigh replied. "Come on over. Jensen and I were just relaxing out on the back deck."

I grabbed my car keys and purse off the kitchen counter. "Good," I said in a rush. "I need to talk to him, too." He'd spent the entire morning with Miles, and I wanted to know what all they talked about.

Everleigh and Jensen only lived about ten minutes away from me, so getting there didn't take long. I parked behind their vehicles and walked up the side steps to their back deck, which was lit by twinkling white lights wrapped around railings. Jensen had put them up at Christmas and never took them down. I was tempted to do the same at my house. Christmas time always had a way of relaxing me; I needed that now.

When I turned the corner, Everleigh was sitting

in her grandmother's favorite rocking chair, rocking back and forth with her hands resting on her belly. She had on a long, white maxi dress with her caramel-blonde hair braided to the side; she looked like an angel. Jensen stood and handed me a small glass of what smelled like whiskey. He held up his glass and clanked it to mine.

"Judging from your call with Everleigh, I figured you needed this."

I laughed and saluted him with the glass. "You have no idea." I downed the amber liquid, which burned the entire way to my stomach.

Jensen took the glass and laughed. "Another?"

I shook my head quickly. "Definitely not."

He set our glasses on the small table between the rocking chairs, each ice cube clinking like a tiny chime. He flourished a hand for me to take his seat, and I accepted with a grateful nod as I sank into the familiar, creaky rocker next to Everleigh. Jensen leaned against the balcony railing, his arms crossed at his chest.

"Okay, tell us what happened," Everleigh said, her voice soft and curious.

My body still hummed with electricity from when Miles kissed me earlier that day. "First," I replied, turning my attention to Jensen. "What did Miles ask you while you were on the boat together this morning?"

Jensen smiled and shook his head. "I didn't tell him anything he didn't need to know. We talked about yours and Everleigh's practice and how great it was going. And he asked a lot of questions about fishing; that was basically it. But I dodged the question when he asked if you were seeing someone. It wasn't my place to tell him."

I nodded thoughtfully. "Yeah, he said you didn't answer. I wouldn't have been mad if you told him."

Jensen sighed and glanced over his shoulder at the dark ocean beyond the balcony. The waves crashed against the shore below in a soothing rhythm.

"I like the guy, Nyla," he finally said, turning back to face me. "He seems very down-to-earth and genuine. He's different from Cohen, the complete opposite, in fact."

"Different as in bad?" I asked him.

Jensen chuckled softly. "No, not bad at all. You just have to figure out what kind of life you want. Miles is a firefighter living in Virginia. He doesn't have the fancy lifestyle that Cohen has. I have no doubt Cohen could give you anything you wanted in the world. It all depends on what makes you happy."

As we sat in silence, the only sounds were the waves and the creaking of the rocking chairs. The night was warm and heavy with the scent of saltwater. I stared out at the vast expanse of ocean before us, wondering what I was going to do. Cohen *could* give me everything I knew Miles couldn't, but I didn't care about material things.

Jensen moved away from the railing and placed a tender kiss on Everleigh's head. "All right, I'm going to leave you two to talk." Everleigh blew him a kiss and winked playfully in response.

"Thanks, Jensen," I said, glancing back at him.

He opened the patio door and smiled warmly. "Anytime. And if you ever want to bring Miles over, he's more than welcome."

He disappeared inside and I turned my attention to Everleigh, who was waving her hands impatiently.

"I need to know what happened," she demanded. "Tell me everything!"

In between deep breaths, I recounted how Miles knew where I was and deliberately planned his work and Luke's bachelor weekend here on purpose. Everleigh squealed with delight, as if this was the most exciting news she had heard.

"So, he wants you back?" I nodded hesitantly and she reached over, squeezing my arm gently in support. "Oh wow, this is wild. What are you going to do? I know how much you loved Miles. I mean, you worked hellish hours at the hospital to get your mind off him."

And did it work? No.

I thought focusing on something else would help

me forget about him. Her eyes were full of sympathy as I leaned my head against the rocking chair and looked up at the stars.

"I don't know what to do," I whispered softly. "I love Miles, but what if our failed marriage was where it was supposed to end?"

Everleigh scoffed and I jerked my attention to her. "Do you really believe that?" she asked, staring at me with raised brows.

I shook my head and averted my gaze back to the sky. I had never believed it. After our divorce, I knew I would've been happy if I'd just given Miles and our marriage the attention they deserved.

"No," I confessed. "I'm not going to lie; I thought my heart was going to leap out of my chest when Miles told me he wanted me back."

"Shouldn't that be the answer you're looking for?"

I turned to Everleigh and sighed. "It should be, but what about Cohen? We haven't been together long, but I can't just throw away the last month as if it didn't exist."

Everleigh nodded in agreement. "You're right. That wouldn't be fair to Cohen." A spark of mischief twinkled in her eyes. "There's only one option then."

My stomach dropped and I groaned; I already knew what she was going to say. "What?" I asked.

Her lips pulled back into a sly grin. "Go out with

both men and see what's there. They might not like it, but it's what you'll have to do."

Yep, that was exactly what I knew would come out of her mouth.

"It was already hard enough telling both men about the other," I said, rubbing my aching chest. The weight of it all felt like it was crushing me. "Imagine what it's going to be like now."

Everleigh chuckled and squeezed my hand reassuringly. "I'm so glad I'm not in your shoes."

"Gee, thanks," I replied sarcastically.

My phone started to ring, and my heart stopped. Everleigh bit her lip and leaned forward. "Is it Cohen?" she asked.

Slowly, I reached into my back pocket and pulled out my phone, seeing Cohen's name on the screen. "It is."

Everleigh shifted in her rocking chair and groaned as she tried to stand. I clutched her arm and helped her up, knowing it couldn't be easy moving around with being in the third trimester.

"Thank you," she said, sounding breathless. "I'm going inside so you can talk to Cohen in private."

Once she walked in, I took a deep breath and accepted the call. "Hey," I answered, trying to keep from sounding like I haven't been in turmoil for the past few hours. "How are you?" I asked him.

"Good. It was a busy day at the office, but things

are wrapping up. I hope to be out of here tomorrow afternoon at the latest."

I walked down the side stairs to the wooden walkway to the beach. "That's good," I said, kicking off my sandals once I got to the sand. The waves crashing against the shore grew louder the closer I got to the water.

"Where are you?" Cohen wondered.

My house was on the sound side of the island where the water was calmer. I glanced back at Everleigh and Jensen's blue cottage. "I'm at Everleigh and Jensen's."

"Oh, I didn't know you were going there tonight. I thought you were going to be with . . ." His voice trailed off and I sighed, already knowing what he was getting at.

"I was," I replied softly, a lump forming in my throat. "After we talked, I wanted to see Everleigh."

The line went silent for a second, but then Cohen cleared his throat before speaking again, only this time his voice was more guarded.

"How did it go? Did you get the closure you wanted?"

I bit my lip so hard it hurt. "Not exactly."

Cohen huffed. "I was right, wasn't I? He wants you back."

The tightness in my chest spread through me.

"He does," I confessed.

Cohen huffed again and I could feel his

frustration radiating through the line. "What are you going to do, Nyla? Do you want to be with him?"

I sat down in the sand, my stomach turning into knots. They grew tighter with every passing second as I weighed my options.

"I don't know, Cohen. I care about you both. You and I have had an amazing month together and I can't just let that go."

Maybe Everleigh was right; I needed to spend time with both Miles and Cohen to see what was truly there. Was I simply clinging to the past I had with Miles? I never doubted his love for me. With Cohen, I had no clue where our relationship could lead. He was an intense man and made it known at every turn that I was his number one focus. I wasn't used to the attention he gave me, but I completely loved it. However, the problem was that I knew Miles would've been the same way if I had let him. And knowing that made the situation I found myself in even harder.

"Why don't you come to New York," Cohen insisted, his voice cutting through the silence. "You need to get away from there. Besides, my parents want to meet you. I can send my private jet to come get you, and we'll be back by Saturday morning before the Spring Fling."

His words caught me off guard. I opened my mouth to speak but then closed it. The only problem with going to New York was that the paparazzi would undoubtedly see me with him. Then, my life would be in the public eye which was what I still didn't want. Judging by the new pictures of Cohen circulating online, the paps were right on his tail the first second he showed his face in the city.

"I'm not ready for that, Cohen. Although, I am impressed about the private jet. I've never been on one before."

I tried to make light of the situation, but it didn't sound like it worked.

"So, I'm going to be sitting here while your ex makes all the moves to get you back?"

My stomach clenched even harder. "I understand it's an awkward situation," I muttered. "I wish I had answers, but I don't know what to do." I took a deep breath and let it out slowly. "If this is too much, I'll understand if you don't want to be around me anymore. You didn't ask for any of this."

Cohen snorted. "You seriously think I'm going to let you go that easily? You've been mine for the past month. I've never been happier. I can't just let someone come in and take that away."

I knew he wouldn't give up. However, a part of me wished he would. I had a feeling Miles and Cohen were going to be relentless.

"Well, be prepared," I warned. "You're not the only one who will be bidding for me at the Spring Fling."

Cohen chuckled, but there was nothing

humorous sounding about it. "Good. It's about time I talked with your ex-husband," he growled.

Dread settled into the pit of my stomach. I could only imagine what that conversation was going to be like.

"Great," I replied, my words dripping with sarcasm. "I can't wait."

14

MILES

The morning came all too slowly and the whole pot of coffee did nothing good for my nerves. I didn't want to leave Nyla last night, not with so many things left unsaid, but I couldn't bombard her all at once. Unfortunately, sleep did not come so easily. All I could think about was her in the arms of another man. After I left, did she go and see the other guy? I knew there was a chance she would be involved with someone else, but I was going to do anything and everything I could to get her back. Now that I was here in Oak Island, I couldn't leave without knowing she was mine.

"Dude, did you sleep at all?" Luke asked, yawning as he walked into the living room.

His face was sunburnt from being out on the boat all day from our deep-sea fishing adventure. I finished my last cup of coffee and set the empty mug in the sink.

"Not really," I said, joining him in the living room.

I walked over to the window and peered out at the ocean. The sky was overcast and gray, the exact replica of my mood. I glanced over at Luke, who stared at me with concern.

"Why don't you just text her? There's no point in wondering what's going on in her mind. Just ask her."

His words made me smile. "I'm usually the wise one in the group, not you."

Luke snorted. "Then act like it. Text Nyla."

I grabbed my phone off the coffee table and quickly glanced at the time. It was a little past seven which hopefully meant she wasn't at work yet.

Me: Good morning.

Noah walked into the living room, his face just as red as Luke's, only he had white circles around his eyes where his sunglasses were. He plopped down on the opposite side of the couch from Luke.

"What's up? What are we doing today?"

Luke gestured to me with a mischievous grin on his face. "We're salvaging our best friend's love life." He winked over at Noah. "I told him to text Nyla."

Noah's face lit up. "See if she has any single friends while you're at it."

I shook my head. "You live in Boston, dumb ass. I don't want you hooking up with one of Nyla's friends when you're about to leave."

His gaze narrowed. "What about you? You don't live around here, either. How will that work if you and Nyla decide to work things out?"

Luke and Noah stared at me, their curious gazes never leaving mine. That was a good question, and one I had an answer to, but my phone beeped before I could answer them.

> Nyla: Good morning.

I typed out a quick reply.

> Me: What are you doing after work? Are you going to be with a certain someone else?

A wave of jealousy flooded through me as I imagined all the ways she could be spending her evening with him. My phone beeped, and I closed my eyes, my heart pounding with anticipation.

When I opened my eyes, I read the text.

> Nyla: Actually, no. He's out of town and won't be back until tomorrow night.

"What is she saying?" Luke asked, waving his hands impatiently for me to tell him.

I let out a relieved sigh. "Turns out the other guy's out of town until tomorrow."

Noah jumped to his feet. "This is your time to go for it then! Invite her over tonight. We can order pizza like old times."

Luke chuckled and nodded in agreement. "Do it! Maybe Nyla needs a blast from the past to remember how much fun we all used to have."

And we did.

When Nyla was in college, she was serious about her studies but still carefree. Seeing the way she is now reminds me of those times.

"Here we go," I said, texting her back.

> Me: Do you want to come over to the house and hang out with me and the guys? It'll be like old times.

Her reply came instantly.

> Nyla: Sounds like fun. I'll be there.

I texted her the address to the rental house then set my phone down on the coffee table, and sat in the brown leather seat across from Luke and Noah.

"Are you nervous?" Luke asked, his dark blue eyes studying me closely.

Blowing out a heavy sigh, I leaned my head back

against the chair and rubbed my chest where the ache had been settling for weeks.

"Not nervous," I said quietly. "More like desperate." I peered over at Luke and Noah, who both looked at me expectantly. "There's something you guys don't know." Their brows furrowed as they waited for me to continue. "I knew Nyla was here in Oak Island," I confessed. "It's why I suggested we come here for the bachelor weekend."

They stared at me with shocked expressions. "Why didn't you tell us?" Luke asked incredulously.

I shrugged my shoulders and sighed again. "I didn't want to hear you say I was crazy. Even after our divorce, all I wanted was to work things out with her, but it was impossible after she signed the papers."

Luke's face dropped. "I know that was hard on you. We all thought she'd come to her senses."

I nodded. "And when she signed the papers, I felt like there was no other choice but to go through with it."

Noah shifted in his seat, catching my attention. "Does Nyla know you asked for the divorce in the hope that she'd focus on your marriage instead of her career?"

"Nope," I replied, shaking my head regretfully. "And I can only blame myself for that. I never should've asked for the divorce in the first place. It backfired like hell on me."

Noah leaned forward, his smirk full of mischief. "Hey, do you need me to stay in town as your wingman?"

That made me laugh. "No, I'll be fine. I have two weeks to get her back, and I want to do it alone."

Noah held up his hands. "All right, I understand." He waved back and forth between him and Luke. "You have your best friends for two more days. After that, you're on your own."

"What's really going to be awkward is meeting the other guy. It's bound to happen.

Noah chuckled. "Just don't beat him up."

I turned my gaze toward the window. The ocean seemed so peaceful; its waves crashed gently against the shore and was the complete opposite of how I felt inside. A storm raged inside of me, and I had no clue if I would make it out.

"I'm curious to see what I'm up against," I said more to myself than to them.

Noah snorted again sharply, involuntarily making Luke and I snap our heads toward him. "He's definitely not going to be as handsome as you."

Luke laughed at his response, but I could only stare at the ocean and think. One thing was for sure, I didn't care who the guy was or what he looked like. I was going to put everything on the line to have her be mine again.

15

NYLA

The rental house Miles was staying in was on the opposite end of the island from where I lived. When I pulled up to the house, I parked beside Miles's midnight blue 4Runner and hopped out. The oceanfront house was pale yellow with dark green shutters, sitting on stilts like the rest of the houses on the beach.

"Nyla!" two voices shouted.

I jerked my head up to see Luke and Noah at the top of the stairs, both with sunburned faces. I couldn't help but laugh at Noah's face.

"Nice sunglasses you got there," I joked.

He didn't have any on, but he had white circles around his eyes from where was wearing them. Noah beamed. "Hey, it gives me character."

I laughed. "You already have enough of that."

Unlike Luke, Noah was the party animal; he

could make anyone around him laugh. They rushed down the stairs and Noah snatched me up first, twirling me around. I started to get dizzy and laughed.

"You might want to set me down before I throw up on you."

He dropped me quickly. "Not today."

Luckily, Luke was there to steady me. I hugged him hard and smiled. "I have to say I've missed you guys."

Luke chuckled. "We've missed you, too," he replied, letting me go and staring at me with his deep blue eyes.

A laugh escaped my lips. "You need to tell me about your fiancé. What's her name?" My smile grew wider. "Does your mother like her?" His mother never liked any of the girls he brought home for her to meet.

Luke held up a hand. "First off. Her name's Kristina. And my mom actually likes her. It's shocking since she's never liked any of the others."

"Yes, I know. She liked me, though."

Luke snorted. "That's because you were in school to be a doctor. That's the kind of woman she wanted me with."

We reached the top of the stairs, and I stopped to face him. I didn't realize how much I missed talking to him.

"What does Kristina do?"

His eyes sparkled as he pulled out his phone to show me a picture of a woman with long dark hair and a kind smile, surrounded by a golden retriever and nine puppies.

"She's a vet," he said, grinning at the picture a few seconds more before putting his phone away. "We have three dogs at home. I have a feeling there might be more when I get back."

Noah came up behind me, his voice by my ear. "You still like all the toppings on your pizza, right? Or did you turn vegan on us?" I looked back at him, and he offered me a crooked grin before winking.

I laughed. "I still eat meat, Noah."

"Good, because that's what we ordered you!" He disappeared inside, leaving me alone with Luke.

"So, where's the ceremony going to be?" I asked.

He glanced toward the horizon and smiled. "Hampshire House."

My jaw dropped and I exhaled a gasp of amazement. "Wow. That's fancy."

Hampshire House was the perfect venue for a wedding with its romantic ambiance and elegant décor; just one step into that place made you feel like royalty.

"Yeah, I know," he said, focusing back on me. "Kristina's mom and dad wanted her to have her dream wedding, and that's where she picked. All I needed to know was the date and time to be there."

Miles and I didn't have the financial means to get

married in a place like that. Nevertheless, I was content with how we got married; the pictures were tucked away in a box in my closet. I hadn't opened it since the divorce.

I lightly touched Luke's arm with my palm. "I'm so happy for you, Luke."

He beamed brightly at me. "Hey, do you want to come? I'd love to have you at the wedding; it's in three weeks."

Excitement bubbled in my veins. "I would love to go. Let me see if I can take the time off."

He pulled out his phone. "Good. I'll get Kristina to send you an invitation. What's your address?"

I recited it off to him and he sent it to her. A few seconds later, his phone beeped, and his grin widened. "Done. She's putting it in the mail tomorrow."

"Are you two going to stay out here all night, or are you coming inside?"

Miles stood in the doorway, his silhouette framed by the warm glow of the living room. His blue T-shirt was tight enough to highlight his broad shoulders and muscular arms, and I had to take a deep breath to steady my racing heart. He flashed me that same mischievous grin he had when we first met ten years ago, and I could feel the familiar butterflies dancing in my stomach.

Luke stepped around me to get inside, and Miles waved an inviting hand for me to do the same. The moment I crossed the threshold, the smell of pizza hit me like a wall and my stomach rumbled hungrily.

Miles chuckled and shut the patio door behind us. "Can you still eat a whole medium pizza by yourself?"

I turned to him with a playful grin. "You better believe it. We might have to go on a long walk afterward so I can burn off some of it."

Luke and Noah snickered knowingly, their minds undoubtedly going to more dirty thoughts. There was a time when Miles and I would work off our calories in other ways, but I couldn't let my mind venture to that.

What was bad was that I really wanted to.

WE FINISHED EATING AND, true to my word, I polished off my entire medium pizza. It was something I hadn't done in many years and I suspect my stomach was going to pay for it later.

We played a few rounds of poker for old times' sake, but as soon as the sun started to go down, Miles and I decided to go for a walk on the beach. The sand was still warm from the afternoon sun, but the further you stuck your toes in, you could feel the coolness. It was April, which was the time of year when some days would be hot and some chilly.

The other day, I saw a picture online that

predicted the weather in North Carolina accurately. It was of a man who, in the first picture, was wearing a jacket and pants for the morning, and when it got to lunch, he was in short sleeves and shorts. By the afternoon, he was in only shorts, his body covered in sweat and holding a fan. Then, when the sun goes down at night, you'd have to be bundled up again. However, that was only for the spring and fall seasons. Summertime could be pretty brutal with all the humidity.

Miles walked close to my side, our arms sometimes brushing against each other. Every time we touched, it took all I had not to smile.

"Tonight was fun," I said, looking over at him.

He smiled and nodded. "It was. I hate that the guys have to leave so soon. They were excited about seeing you."

"Same," I said. "Although I guess I can't be too shocked that Noah hasn't changed one bit. He's still as wild as ever. I thought for sure he'd find a nice girl and settle down."

Miles focused his gaze to the sand. "He will one day. Right now, he's enjoying life. Some of us consider finding that special someone to be more important than others."

Thinking of Luke and how he was getting married soon made me think of mine and Miles's wedding.

"Luke told me that he and Kristina are getting married at Hampshire House."

Miles chuckled and turned his blue gaze my way. "That's nice, right? I wish I could've given you something like that."

Hearing that hurt my heart. I linked my arm with his and his eyes flashed with need at my touch. The warmth of his skin made goose bumps fan out over my skin; I loved the excitement of it.

"I didn't need a fancy wedding, Miles. Getting married in my parents' backyard was perfect enough. We had everything we needed. All our friends were there, and we had cake."

Miles tilted his head back and laughed; I knew I could get him to smile at that.

"Still. There was so much I wish I could've given you."

I held his arm tighter. "I had everything I needed. I just didn't know it until it was too late."

"That goes for both of us, Nyla," he said, his voice full of trepidation.

We walked slowly, and I wanted to enjoy every single second. Being with Miles was like being at home; I felt comfortable, safe. But it was also exciting and new. Nothing was ever dull with Miles. The passion was always off the charts and that made things interesting.

"Were you serious about going to Luke and Kristina's wedding?" he asked, furrowing his brows.

I nodded excitedly. "I wouldn't want to miss it." My smile faded and I bit my lip. "But I have a question." He cocked his head to the side, waiting for me to continue. "Are your parents going to be there?" I wondered.

Miles raised an eyebrow at me before smirking devilishly. "Yes. Why do you ask?"

Sheepishly, I bit my lip again. "Do they hate me?"

He burst out laughing. "Oh yeah, they despise you. I'd be afraid of my mom dumping the punch all over you."

I pulled away from him and smacked his arm. "That's not funny. Tell me the truth."

Miles chuckled again and shook his head. "No, they don't hate you. They know I'm here to see you."

I gasped in surprise. "They do? So, does that mean your mother *won't* be pouring punch all over me? I have a pretty green dress that I'd love to wear, but I don't want it to get ruined."

Miles moved closer to me, our arms touching again, but I made no move to hold onto him this time, even though I wanted to.

"My parents were more pissed at me over our divorce than anyone," he confessed.

"Why?" I asked.

He stopped walking and stepped in front of me, his expression serious. "They were mad because I asked for the divorce when I didn't want it. They disapproved of my method."

His words confused me. "Your method? What are you talking about?"

He glanced up at the darkened sky and sighed. "It was a test, Nyla. I only filed for divorce to see if I could grab your attention."

My heart stopped and the tears in my eyes burned hotter than anything I'd ever felt. Even my lungs burned as if I couldn't get enough oxygen. I remember the day I received the divorce papers. I had just gotten home from working over sixty hours at the hospital, and they were waiting for me on the kitchen table. The house was quiet, but I remembered hearing my heart breaking as I opened the large envelope. Miles had decided to stay at the fire station that night. It was one of the loneliest nights of my life. I'd signed the papers, and the next day, I found an apartment and moved my things out. I was ashamed for letting my job get in the way of our marriage. At the time, it felt like it was too late to do anything about it.

There was no stopping the tears from cascading down my cheeks.

"I thought it was what you wanted, so I signed them," I whispered. "I knew I'd screwed up. And instead of working things out, I submerged myself in more work." I turned away from him and angrily wiped the tears from my eyes. "I was so stupid. I literally hate myself for being such an idiot. Saying I'm sorry isn't good enough."

Miles wrapped his arms around my waist, and my whole body melted into him. "I don't want an apology, Nyla. All I've ever wanted was your heart."

"It's always been with you, Miles."

Miles turned me around in his arms. "Then why can't you just end it with this other guy and be with me? I know we can make this work."

Sighing, I stepped out of his hold and peered out at the ocean. "He's a good person, Miles. It pains my heart to think of hurting him like I hurt you. I can't just end it over the phone."

He scoffed. "You also can't let guilt be why you stay with him, Nyla."

"I'm not," I said, turning to face him. "But what about us? How do you plan on making this work? You live in Virginia!" I released a heavy sigh. "And I have my practice here. It's been a dream come true having my own place. I don't . . ."

I let my job tear us apart before, but this was different. I didn't want to leave what I had in Oak Island. Miles's lips pulled back slowly, the light in his eyes blazing as he stepped closer.

"I'm not asking you to leave here, Nyla. This is where you belong; it's as clear as day." His calloused hands found mine, and I could feel my heart racing.

"Then what are you asking?" I wondered.

He searched my face with longing in his gaze. "I'm asking that . . ." His words trailed off, and he paused to take a deep breath. "I'm saying that if you want me, I'll pack up everything I have and come here to be with you. I can get a job down here."

It seemed too good to be true. Was it really that simple?

"Just like that?" I asked, feeling dizzy as my heart thundered against my ribcage.

He nodded. "Just like that. We've spent too much time apart. And for what? To be miserable? I don't want to live like that anymore." He pulled me closer, his lips so close to mine. "I need you in my life, Nyla. I told myself I'd do anything to get you back, and I meant it. Whatever you want me to do, I'll do it."

Lifting my hands, I cupped his cheeks. "I'm the reason things didn't work, Miles. It should be me doing everything I can to be with you."

He leaned into my touch, his blue gaze burning with passion; it made my whole body tremble.

"There *is* something you can do."

And I knew what that was. I slid my hands away from his face.

"I'm going to talk to him when he comes back. But you have to know that he's loved in this town. My friends adore him. It's not like he's going to go away."

Miles's jaw clenched and he nodded. "Then we'll deal with it. All I want is for you to be mine again."

That was all I wanted too, but I had to break the news to Cohen first before I let anything progress with Miles.

16

"We seriously have a ton of stuff," Autumn said, laughing as she looked around the room.

Our entire waiting room was filled with boxes of goodies for the Spring Fling tomorrow. Luckily, we didn't schedule any patients for this Friday afternoon so we could prepare. We needed the time.

Autumn had all the different boxes opened, revealing the contents inside each one. We had avocado-shaped stress balls, pens, sticky pads, notepads, and small first aid kits in plastic containers with the Seaside Family Practice logo on them. Everyone who decides to stop by our table tomorrow will get a bag filled with all of it. Gina and Autumn started loading the bags with each item, and I also pitched in.

According to past Spring Fling attendance

records, there had always been thousands of guests, and this year was projected to have more people. By the time we were almost done, over half the room was covered in a sea of plastic gift bags.

Autumn cleared her throat and when I looked over at her, I could tell there was something she wanted to ask.

"What is it, Autumn?"

She tossed a first aid kit into her last gift bag and piled it with all the others. "Just curious, is all. You haven't said much about the time you've been spending with your ex-husband."

I finished filling up my last bag and just smiled at her. Autumn jerked her head over to Gina and waved a hand frantically in the air. "Why is she grinning like that? Do you know what it means?" she asked Gina.

Gina chuckled and winked over at me with playful amusement. "I think the doctor has figured out what her heart wants."

I held up a hand, halting her. "I may know what I want, but I'm not doing anything about it until Cohen gets back in town."

Autumn squealed and jumped to her feet. "So, you're picking the sexy firefighter ex-husband?"

As if on cue, the door opened and there stood Miles, grinning devilishly with a pink bakery box in his hands. It was apparent he'd heard what Autumn had said. He looked around, taking in the many gift bags piled on the floor before turning back to us.

"Wow. You guys have been busy. Is this for the festival tomorrow?" I stood to join him, staring at the bakery box curiously.

"We took the afternoon off so we could prepare." I gestured to the covered floor. "I didn't realize how much work it would be."

"If I'd have known you were doing that I would have helped," he offered.

I waved him off. "It's okay. We got it done."

He handed over the pink bakery box and smiled. "Maybe these will help."

I opened the box and inside were a dozen chocolate-covered cake pops. Autumn came over and smiled like a kid in a candy store when she looked at them.

Giggling, I held the box out. "Go ahead and have some."

She snatched up two and thanked Miles at least a dozen times. Gina grabbed a couple and even I couldn't resist. I set the box down on the front desk and bit into the chocolatey goodness, loving how the cake pop melted in my mouth.

"Thank you. This is the perfect afternoon treat."

Miles sat down on one of the waiting room chairs and smiled. "I ran into Jensen at the marina this morning. He said you and Everleigh love cake pops. Apparently, your friend, Michelle, got you hooked on them."

"That's true," I said, loving the warmth that blossomed through my chest. "What were you doing at the marina?"

He shrugged. "I was walking through town and thought I'd look at the boats. Jensen was out there getting ready to take a group of guys out fishing. He said he's not taking long jobs again until after Everleigh has their baby."

I nodded. "That's right. He doesn't want to risk not being here when the baby's born."

Miles's gaze dropped to my stomach, and he smiled before meeting my eyes again. There was a time when we talked about having children, but I was too busy with work even to consider it. Now, things have changed; I would love to have a family.

"I would be the same way," he admitted.

Autumn and Gina smiled at each other as they finished their cake pops.

"You two are more than welcome to go home," I told them. "The bags are done and there's really nothing left to do."

Autumn glanced at her watch and smiled. "You don't have to tell me twice. It's still early in the afternoon, too. I might head out to the beach and get some sun."

Gina chuckled and ruffled Autumn's blonde hair.

"Oh, to be young again. I'm going home to get dinner started early."

"I'll see you tomorrow, ladies," I called out as they disappeared down the hall to the back door.

When I joined Miles again in the waiting room, he stood and gestured toward all the bags on the floor. "Do you need help setting up tomorrow? Luke and Noah just left to return to Boston, but I know they would've helped too if they were here."

"Oh no," I said, hating that they left without saying goodbye. "I wish I could've seen them one last time before they headed out."

Miles nodded in agreement. "Me too, but they knew you were working and didn't want to bother you. But," he said, his lips pulling back into a grin, "you'll see them in three weeks at the wedding. It's going to be a good time." He pointed at all the stuff on the floor. "But again, do you need help tomorrow morning?"

It just so happened that Jensen and Cohen were supposed to help me and the girls set up. What shocked me was that he didn't call last night, which was strange for him. A part of me felt guilty for all the time I'd spent with Miles behind Cohen's back. Miles only kissed me that one time, and he knew I didn't want things to go further until everything was settled. Still, I dreaded seeing Cohen and telling him everything that had happened. I never expected Miles to come back into my life and turn my world on its axis. It was something I'd always wanted, and I just didn't realize how hard it would hit me until I saw him in that parking lot.

"As much as I'd love your help, I don't know if it'll be wise," I said, biting my lip nervously.

Miles's grin faded and he sighed. "Let me guess, lover boy's supposed to help you?"

I rolled my eyes. "I think so. He and Jensen had planned on it weeks ago. It's just I haven't spoken to him. He didn't call last night."

Miles lifted his brows. "What do you think is going on?"

I shrugged. "Not sure. He's supposed to get back tonight."

He cleared his throat, his gaze narrowed. "And are you going to tell him about us when he does?"

My chest tightened with dread. "That's my plan. I feel so bad about it." By the smug grin on his face, it was obvious he found too much joy in it. "You don't have to look so happy about it," I said, pursing my lips.

He shrugged. "I know I shouldn't feel that way. But I know how any man could fall for you all too well. Guess I should feel sorry for the guy."

I walked over to the box of cake pops and closed it up. "If I need your help setting up, I'll be sure to call," I assured him.

Miles chuckled from behind me. "Don't worry.

I'll still be there. I have to see who my competition is for the auction."

I picked up the box and turned to face him. "I'm so ready for tomorrow to come and go."

Miles winked. "I just hope I win the grand prize. If not, at least the money's going to a good cause."

The two charities I chose to send the proceeds to are CancerCare and the Breast Cancer Research Foundation. My mom had been diagnosed with breast cancer a few years ago, but she was lucky enough to beat it.

"How's your mom been doing?" Miles asked. "Everything good with her health?"

"She's great," I replied, remembering the last time my parents had come to visit. They had such a blast that I was sure they would eventually move down here. "My parents like it here," I told him. "I keep waiting for them to say they're buying a house close by."

Miles smiled and shook his head. "Hopefully, they will. You'll have everything here if they do."

"What about you?" I wondered. "You said you'd move down here to be with me. Are you still planning on doing that?"

Miles leaned in, his eyes piercing mine with an intense longing that sent shivers down my spine. "I'm waiting on you to say the words. When you want me to move, I will."

Even though I knew I wanted to be with him, it

was too soon to plan it. We still needed time together to get to know each other again as we were both different people than the ones we were when we were still married.

Miles waited patiently for my response, so I squeezed his hand.

"We'll figure it out together."

We stared at each other, and it was so easy to get lost in his eyes. But then, the sound of children squealing with delight broke the trance.

Miles laughed and nodded toward the door. "Sounds like they're having fun. What do you say we go find something to do since you're done with work for the day?"

Excitement coursed through every fiber of my being. "That sounds great to me."

It was still early in the afternoon, and we had plenty of time to do all sorts of things. However, there was one place on my mind that would be perfect.

"I know where we can go," I said, clutching the box of cake pops in my arms. "And we have these awesome treats to keep us company on the way."

Miles cocked his head to the side, his expression curious. "Where do you want to go?"

I nodded toward the door. "Airlie Gardens in Wilmington. It's about an hour's drive, but it's a beautiful place."

Miles took the box of treats from me and stepped out of the way. "Let's go. My car's out front."

I walked quickly through the office to ensure everything was turned off and the back door was locked. I grabbed my purse and traveling medical bag before following Miles out the front door and locking it behind me. He had the passenger's side door of his 4Runner open for me, a vivid reminder of how many times we'd done this same thing in the past.

"Has your taste in music changed these past two years?" he asked, hands stuffed into his pockets with a smirk playing at his lips.

I shook my head. "Nope. I still like the same old stuff."

He nodded toward the seat, and then once we were both inside, he started up the engine—sending an all-too-familiar song ringing through the speakers. "My Sweet Summer" by The Dirty Heads. We saw them at our first concert together about nine years ago.

I looked over at Miles and smiled. "So many memories."

He chuckled and nodded. "All good ones."

Yes, they were.

iles and I walked around the gardens and talked the entire time. It was as if no time had passed between us. We were still the same two people we were all those years ago, except now we were older and more mature. I knew what I needed in life to be happy; my priorities were finally straight.

"What would you say our best vacation was?" I asked, opening up the bakery box to grab a cake pop.

After walking several miles at the gardens, I'd worked up an appetite. We were already in the car, headed back to Oak Island, and the traffic was horrendous. It was definitely going to take a lot longer to get back.

Miles narrowed his gaze in concentration and blew out a breath. "I'm thinking Wyoming when we went to Jackson Hole and hiked all those trails in the Grand Teton National Park."

I nodded in agreement. We went there in early May about five years ago, and there was still snow on the trails. The mountains were breathtaking.

"Same. I had a blast that trip, even though I got doused with muddy rainwater when we walked to breakfast that morning."

Since our hotel was a short distance from so many great restaurants, Miles and I liked to walk instead of drive. One morning after a heavy rainfall, we still decided to walk. While on the sidewalk, a car drove through a massive puddle beside me; I got soaked.

Miles tilted his head back and laughed. "I remember. I wanted to beat the hell out of the asshole who did that to you."

I did, too.

"At least until we saw who it was," I said, grinning happily.

Miles chuckled again. "Who would've thought it would be Hadley Rivers?"

I wasn't a country music listener, but everyone who did knew who Hadley Rivers was; she was one of the top country singers in the world. She apologized a million times over and paid for our breakfast that morning. When we got back to our hotel, it turned out that she'd paid for our entire stay, and even brought new clothes to our room for me. To say it was my favorite trip was an understatement.

"Her paying for our hotel room helped us out. I swear, I never thought I would ever pay off my school loans."

Miles snorted. "True, but we got it done. Even though we didn't have money back then, we still managed to do everything we wanted."

"We didn't need money to be happy," I said in a low voice, whispering it more at myself than to him.

Miles reached over and intertwined his fingers with mine. "That's because we had each other."

But then, things changed when I started working at the hospital. I wanted to earn money, find my place in the medical world, and pay off my debts. The admiration I got from being one of the best ER doctors in the state became an addiction, and I wanted to constantly prove myself even more. I'd give anything to go back and change how I did things.

Miles's thumb slowly rubbed soothing circles on my wrist, and I looked up into his eyes—there was the familiar twinkle that always brought a flood of warmth to my heart.

"Do you think we'd be where we are now if we stayed together?"

His smile faded slightly as he paused for a beat before responding. "I don't know, Nyla. I would love to say yes, but I tend to lean on the side that everything happens for a reason. All I know is that I have never seen you this happy before. And it just so happens that I'm here with you."

Miles concentrated back on the road, and I noticed a lot of traffic up ahead. Pulling out my phone, I looked for any alternate routes back to Oak Island. It just so happened there was one that was mainly back roads; only it added an extra ten minutes to the trip.

"Do we want to stay on this road or go the long, country road route?" I asked. "If you want no traffic, you can take a right on that road up ahead." I pointed at it and he got over in the right lane.

"Let's go the back way. I don't mind if it's a little longer."

I smiled over at him. "Neither do I."

The more time I spent with him, the harder it felt like I was falling. I never thought I'd feel this alive again.

When we turned down the back road, it was pretty desolate, which was nice. There was a long road ahead of us with no cars in sight.

Miles cleared his throat. "There's still some fish left over that I need to cook. Want to come over and eat dinner together?"

As much as I wanted to say yes, I knew it wasn't a good idea yet. I still hadn't spoken to Cohen. I wanted to talk to him before letting things progress with Miles.

With a heavy sigh, I turned my head toward Miles and leaned against the seat. "Not tonight," I said, watching the disappointment flicker across his face. "Tomorrow's a busy day for me. I know how you and I can get sometimes. We'll be up till all hours talking, and then I'll be a zombie at the Spring Fling."

His smile came back, and he nodded in understanding. "That's true. I remember us doing that the first night we met."

As memories of that fateful evening resurfaced, I couldn't help but smile. Miles had been my savior, my knight in shining armor. I remembered how he had looked that night: tall and handsome, with his sexy bedhead blond hair and piercing eyes. The drunkard at the bar had been relentless, trying to buy me drinks despite repeated rejections. He was getting handsy and just as I was about to knee him in a painful place, Miles appeared out of nowhere and claimed to be my boyfriend. His voice was like thunder as he threatened to dismember the drunk if he didn't back off. The guy scurried away like a scared rabbit and Miles stayed by my side for the rest of the night.

"You were my hero," I confessed.

Miles smirked over at me. "I'm so glad I was there to help."

That night was also the first time I'd met Noah. He and my roommate hit it off quickly so both he and Miles came to our apartment and stayed the night. While my roommate and Noah had fun in her bedroom, Miles and I watched TV all night in the living room. It wasn't just his bravery that drew me to him, though; we talked until we watched the sun rise over the city skyline. We shared stories of our dreams and fears, our likes and dislikes, and everything in between. That night felt like fate had brought us together.

"We talked about so much that night," I murmured.

Miles kept his eyes on the road and smiled. "We did. And the next morning, I had to go to work. It's a good thing there weren't any major fires."

I waved him off. "You would've been fine. I don't know anyone with the same work ethic as you. You were always a hard worker."

Even when he was sick, he never missed a day of work. I was the same way.

Miles smiled over at me. "I still haven't called in sick yet. At some point, I need to take all my vacation days. I think I have three months of days to take off."

My mouth dropped in shock. "Wow. You might want to get on that."

He winked. "I was thinking about it."

There was no denying the spark of excitement that coursed through my body. He was supposed to stay in Oak Island for another couple of weeks for work, but it would be nice if he could stay longer. Everything between us was so up in the air. I had no clue what was going to happen once Cohen came back into town and things got complicated. I didn't want to hurt him, but I had a feeling it was going to be inevitable.

"What's on your mind, Ny?" Miles asked.

I focused on the road and opened my mouth to speak, but I didn't want to talk about Cohen. Once tomorrow comes and they meet at the Spring Fling, I had no doubt there would be a lot of awkward conversations from everyone. The people around town knew I was with Cohen, but soon, they were going to find out about Miles. It was like I was in a soap opera, stuck in the middle of two lovers.

"Nyla?" Miles called out, glancing quickly over at me.

I laughed and shook my head. "I have way too much on my mind."

We came up behind a white SUV, but were still a little way behind them when all of a sudden, they slammed down on their brakes just as three deer darted across the road. Everything happened so fast after that. Their vehicle swerved back and forth, clearly out of control; I knew it was going to flip over. My heart stopped as I watched in terror as the inevitable happened. The SUV flipped over three times and landed in the embankment; thankfully, right side up. The sound of it all was going to stay imprinted in my mind for a long time.

Adrenaline shot through me like a rocket, spurring me into action. I wanted to help them. Miles gripped the steering wheel and pulled over, his expression focused and determined. After I called 9-1-1 and quickly explained everything, I grabbed my traveling medical bag out of the back seat. I kept the line open with the dispatcher but put it on speaker and slid my cell into my back pocket. Talking to them was not as important as trying to save the people's lives in the SUV. All that mattered was that help was on the way. Until then, I was going to do everything in my power to save the people in the car. They were going to be lucky if they were still alive.

Miles and I leaped out of his car, and my feet skidded across the pavement as we raced toward the SUV. Its airbags had all been deployed, and its windows were smashed, leaving a glittery trail of glass shards around it.

The girl in the driver's seat had blood streaming down her face from an open wound on her forehead, while the guy in the passenger seat was slumped over with a deep gash on his arm, dripping red. Miles tugged at the driver's door handle and helped me carry the female out of the ravaged vehicle and onto the ground.

"Do you need help with him?" I shouted over my shoulder as Miles ran back to the car.

"No! You work on her. I got this!" he hollered back.

I removed my medical kit, carefully inspected her wound, and applied a sterile dressing to protect it from contamination. Suddenly, her honey-colored eyes fluttered open wide with fear and confusion. She attempted to sit up, but I gently guided her back onto the ground. Immediately she glanced at her car and let out a pained cry.

"Oh my God . . . Brian! Where's my husband? Is he okay?"

"He'll be fine," I murmured, continuing to bandage up her head carefully. There was also a gash on her shoulder which was oozing blood. The more she moved, the more she bled. "Just stay still," I said, keeping my voice calm and soft. "Help is on the way. What's your name?"

She closed her eyes and tears fell down her face and into her light warm brown hair. "Emily. My name's Emily."

I glanced over at Miles, who had Brian on the ground. My heart sank when I watched him take Brian's pulse, and a pained expression passed across his face. Miles got into position and looked at me quickly; all I could do was nod. He started CPR and I sent a silent prayer to the heavens, begging for help.

"I want to see Brian!" Emily demanded, trying to look his way.

I moved into her line of sight so she couldn't see

Miles working on him. Tears stung my eyes, but I concentrated on her wounds.

"You have a wound on your shoulder that needs to be cleaned. I'm a doctor. Just stay still for me," I ordered.

Emily was on the verge of a hysterical panic attack, and I could see it about to burst free. It was clear how much she loved Brian and couldn't rest until she knew he was okay. I saw so much of myself in her because I would've been the same way. I could hear Miles faintly counting out his repetitions, which was the last thing Emily needed to hear. She needed to be calmed down before the wound on her shoulder opened further. I started to hum, and then, out of nowhere, I was singing the words to a Celine Dion song. With Gina singing them every day while at the office, it was hard not to remember them.

Emily stared at me as I sang to her while bandaging her shoulder. After a few seconds, she joined in, and it seemed to calm her. Soon, I had her wound dressed, but the blood was seeping through the cloth. Emily started to cry again, but I cupped her cheeks, gently rubbing her tears away.

"Shh, it's okay. Tell me about Brian. Do you have kids?"

Emily nodded and closed her eyes. I took time to look over my shoulder; Miles was still performing CPR.

"We've been married two years," Emily

whispered, grimacing in pain. The adrenaline of the crash had to be wearing off. She sniffled and opened her eyes. "We're trying to have kids. I'm two weeks late and I was going to take a test when we got home."

I slid my hands off her face and carefully held her hands. "That's amazing news, Emily," I murmured, trying to keep my own tears at bay.

Her lips trembled and more tears fell. "What if I'm pregnant? What if the baby's not okay?"

I gently squeezed her hands. "Help is on the way. You're going to be taken care of."

Just then, I heard a strangled gasp for air, and my heart jumped. I quickly looked over my shoulder and Brian's eyes were open, his chest heaving up and down. Miles had a hand on his shoulder and Brian turned our way, clearly searching for Emily. I moved out of the way so he could see her and she could see him. Their eyes locked and she let out a relieved sigh. She mouthed the words "I love you" to him and he did the same to her.

In the distance, the sirens blared, and it wasn't long before the whole road was filled with ambulances, police cars, and fire trucks. Everything was going to be okay.

I watched Emily and Brian get loaded into their ambulances and whisked away with the lights blaring. Out of all my years as a firefighter, I'd never had to perform CPR on anyone. When I didn't feel Brian's pulse, I didn't even hesitate. I knew what I had to do, and I was going to do everything in my power to save him.

Once the police officers and the medical crews heard my and Nyla's side of the story, they left us on our own. However, before we could go, several news vans pulled up and they were directed to us after speaking with the police. I felt a bead of sweat roll down the back of my neck as the reporters crowded around us, shoving microphones in our faces. My mind was still reeling from everything that just happened.

One of the reporters, a tall woman with a shock

of dark brown hair, leaned in close. "Can you tell us what happened here today?" she asked, her expression curious.

I hesitated momentarily before nodding, feeling Nyla's comforting hand on my shoulder. "We were riding behind the victims' SUV, and they must've been startled when some deer ran out into the road. They lost control of their car, and we watched it flip about three times before going into the embankment." I looked over at Nyla and sighed before turning back to the cameras. "We pulled the victims out of the car and tended to them before the paramedics came."

The reporter brought her microphone back to her mouth. "One of the officers said you saved the male victim, that you performed CPR on him. Is that true?"

I nodded in response. "I did. I'm a firefighter and I knew what I had to do." Reaching down, I grabbed Nyla's hand. "Dr. Nyla Clark here helped the female victim. She had some nasty gashes that Dr. Clark treated. I'm just glad we were able to help."

The reporter nodded and beamed at us. "You two are heroes. The victims are lucky you were close by."

She focused on the camera and wrapped up the interview. We answered a few more questions from the other reporters, which lasted over half an hour. The adrenaline I had pounding through me earlier had left me, and all I was feeling now was mental exhaustion. The same thing went for Nyla, judging by how she leaned into me for support as we walked back to my 4Runner.

I opened the passenger's side door for her and she stepped forward, throwing her arms around my neck. I could feel her heart beating against my own as I pulled her into a tight embrace, breathing in the sweet scent of her strawberry perfume that seemed to linger around her.

"What if we weren't here?" she whispered, her breath warm and close against my neck. "Brian wouldn't have made it."

I ran my hand soothingly down her back, searching for the right words to assure her. "But we were. Things happen for a reason, Nyla. I have to believe we were meant to be on this road today. We saved two lives."

Nyla's arms slowly slid away from me and she stepped back, looking up at me with a tired smile. "How does it feel?" she said softly.

Saving people was nothing new to me; in my work as a firefighter, I had previously pulled many out of burning buildings. But Brian had no pulse when I'd started CPR; knowing his only chance lay with me had been terrifying.

"When I'm not crashing from an adrenaline rush," I told her honestly, "I'll let you know how it feels. But I'm sure it will feel pretty damn good."

Nyla squeezed my arm in understanding. "It will.

When I worked in the ER, it felt amazing when I saved people. But it also killed me when I couldn't."

And I knew that better than anyone. Sometimes she'd come home and cry in the shower when she lost one of her patients. Nyla always had too big of a heart to disassociate herself from the patients.

Nyla climbed in the car, and I pulled away from the edge of the road. The tow truck had just taken Emily and Brian's SUV away, but there were still remnants of glass scattered across the asphalt. The sun had set, and the night sky was a deep navy blue. We drove in silence for a few minutes until I heard her stomach growl.

"Are you sure you don't want me to cook for you?" I asked.

Nyla rolled her head back against the seat and released a yawn. "How about a rain check? I do know I could use a drink and some chocolate right about now."

We both laughed, but hers was tinged with exhaustion. "Sounds good to me," I replied.

We stopped at a diner on the way back into Oak Island and grabbed a to go order of cheeseburgers, waffle fries, and milkshakes. We both had our food eaten by the time we pulled into her driveway.

"Do you want me to come here in the morning to take you to get your car?"

She had left it at her office to ride with me to Wilmington, but it was late and I knew she was drained. The last thing I wanted was for her to get in an accident.

Nyla shook her head and opened her door. "Don't worry about it. I'm sure Jensen and Everleigh won't mind stopping by here."

Or was the other guy going to pick her up and she didn't want to tell me? I didn't even know his name. Maybe it was a good thing I didn't. It almost made me believe he wasn't even real. All I knew was that he hadn't called her in over a day. Was that good for me? I could only hope so.

I walked Nyla up to her door and her phone started to vibrate in her purse. Jealousy threatened to wash over me because I figured it'd be the other guy, but I pushed the feelings down when I noticed the name "Everleigh" on the screen. I didn't want to be jealous of the other guy, but it was hard not to be. While answering the call, she opened the door with one hand and gestured for me to come inside. After following her into the kitchen, she grabbed a cold beer from the refrigerator, handed it to me, and led me into the living room.

We both sat on her couch, and I listened as she told Everleigh about the car accident and everything that happened after. Apparently, we had been on several news stations. When she hung up the phone with Everleigh, it rang again almost immediately; this time, it was Autumn. She spent the next hour talking to people from the town who were full of questions, mainly wanting to know who I was. She answered truthfully, even though I knew she didn't want everyone to know. When she hung up with the last person, she shut off her phone, and laid her head back on the couch.

"Well, it looks like the secret is out."

"What do you mean?" I asked.

She closed her eyes and breathed a deep sigh. "You and me," she replied. "Everyone knows you're my ex-husband. I have a feeling they're all making their assumptions right now."

"Does that bother you?"

Her face softened into a weary expression as she slowly opened her heavy eyelids to look at me. "No, not really. It's just if they saw the news, I have no doubt word is going to spread even more. I didn't want us being together to be publicized like that before I had time to—"

I held up a hand, nodding my understanding. "I get it. You don't want your friend finding out anything before you get a chance to talk to him face-to-face."

"Yeah," she whispered, curling her legs onto the couch. "He deserves the truth from me, not to hear rumors from other people." A small smile spread across her face. "One good thing about today is that you're the town hero. Everyone is dying to meet you tomorrow. I think we should have *you* as the prize tomorrow for the auction instead of me."

Her eyes started to flutter shut, and I softly ran my fingers along the curve of her jawline and gently pushed back a single strand of her bright red hair behind her ear.

"You're much prettier than I am," I teased. "I wouldn't bring in nearly as much money for your charities as you can. Besides," I said, letting my hand slide off her skin. "You're a town hero, too. I wouldn't have been able to calm Emily down the way you did."

She breathed in deeply and let it out, her body relaxing into the couch. "Yeah, but you brought someone back to life. That is something special." Her head started to droop. "*You* are special."

It was only a matter of seconds before sleep completely took her. Gently, I scooped her into my arms and carried her to her bedroom. I laid her on the bed and took off her shoes, trying my best not to wake her. Once she was tucked in, I resisted the urge to kiss her and turned for the door.

I was way past ready for her to be mine again.

19

NYLA

I woke up to the sun shining on my face and dressed in yesterday's clothes. At first, I couldn't even remember how I ended up in bed and assumed Miles carried me there. The last thing I could recall was sitting on the couch with Miles and trying desperately to stay awake. I'd had a gazillion phone calls and I was exhausted.

Groaning, I laid back on my pillow. Today was going to be a long, awkward day. Luckily, it was only seven-thirty in the morning, so I had plenty of time to shower and prepare for the Spring Fling. I slid out of bed and searched for my phone; it was exactly where I remembered leaving it on the couch.

When I turned it on, it dinged over a dozen times with missed texts and phone calls. My heart sank when I saw that there was a voice mail from Cohen. I had no clue what was going on with him.

Biting my lip, I pressed the play button and listened to his voice through the phone. "Nyla, it's me. I've tried calling you a few times tonight. I just wanted to make sure you were okay. I've had some extra things to take care of here in New York, which has put me back a day. I was hoping to get home to you tonight, but it's looking like I won't make it until late tomorrow morning. But don't worry, I'll be there for the Spring Fling. I'm just sorry I can't be there to help you set up. Call me back if you can, but if not, I'll see you soon."

A sense of relief washed through me, but it only delayed the inevitable. Miles and Cohen were going to meet today, and I really wasn't looking forward to it. My heart definitely wasn't ready. Cohen had been so good to me, and the thought of hurting him made me feel terrible. However, there was a light at the end of the tunnel.

In the end, I was going to have Miles back. What did that entail? I had no clue, but it was exciting not knowing. I just knew it was all going to work out in the end.

After taking a quick shower and picking out a sleeveless floral top and jeans for the Spring Fling, I slathered on some makeup and let my hair air dry so it would cascade in waves down my back.

I stared at my phone, wondering if I should call Everleigh and Jensen to pick me up, or call Miles to take him up on his offer to help me this morning.

The whole town already saw him on TV with me, so there was no use in hiding him.

As I entered the kitchen, I made a cup of coffee and forced myself to drink it, hoping the caffeine would soothe my nerves—if anything, it made me more jittery. Still staring at my phone, I quickly ate a muffin and decided just to do what I wanted. I pressed Miles's name and held my breath while waiting for him to pick up.

"Good morning, sunshine," he said.

Hearing his voice made goose bumps fan out over my skin. "Thank you for not leaving me on the couch last night," I replied.

He chuckled. "You're welcome. I know you used to like taking showers before bed, but I didn't want to wake you. Hope you're not mad at me for that."

"No," I laughed. "I was able to sleep just fine."

I always loved night showers because they helped me relax after a long day at the ER. My life wasn't as hectic as it used to be, so I didn't need the nightly showers as much anymore.

"It's crazy how we remember quirks like that, isn't it?" I said.

"It is," he agreed, his voice almost sad. "There were times when you'd get in bed thinking I was asleep and run your fingers through my hair. Whenever you touched me like that, I tried to hold onto how it made me feel. When I doubted your love, I thought of moments like that."

Tears burned behind my eyes and I smiled. "It seems so long ago."

Silence filled the air briefly, but then Miles cleared his throat. "Is there a reason you called?"

"Actually, there is," I said, putting my coffee cup in the sink. "I was wondering if you could pick me up and take me to the office. Set up time is about to start for all the vendors."

"What about Jensen? I thought he and your *friend* were supposed to do that for you."

I snorted. "Well, my *friend* is not getting back until late morning. I have a little bit more time before you two meet."

Miles chuckled, but there was no humor to it. "Great. I can't wait. Do you want me to come get you now?"

My heart thudded against my sternum. "If you don't mind."

"All right, I'll be there in a few."

We hung up and about ten minutes later, he pulled into my driveway. The second he got out of his 4Runner, dressed in a light green T-shirt and jeans with mussed up dirty blond hair, our eyes locked and there was a shift in the air between us. He walked toward me, his eyes raking up and down my body. Everything inside of me trembled. He held out his hand and I took it, loving how his warmth seeped into me; my body wanted more.

"You ready for this?"

I shook my head. "Nope, but I'm ready for afterward."

His brows furrowed. "What's happening afterward?"

After talking to Cohen, I would be free to do what I wanted. I looked into Miles's eyes and smiled. I had my ideas, but I was going to let the moment take us wherever it wanted to go.

"I don't know yet," I said, hoping he could see the fire in my eyes, "but I'm looking forward to it."

THE SEASIDE FAMILY Practice table was adorned with brightly colored goodie bags, a large box bearing my photo, and the words "Date with a Doctor" in bold lettering.

While Autumn and Gina walked through the crowds, urging everyone to visit our table, Everleigh and I stayed to represent the Seaside Family Practice. Everleigh had asked the town mayor to stop by at three o'clock to pull out a ticket and announce the winner. People of all ages, local residents, and tourists milled about, grabbing their bags and visiting all the other tables.

My heart warmed as I watched grown men and women, boys and girls, line up to buy tickets for the auction box. Several of the women had breast cancer, or had survived it, and were happy to see some of the money going toward the Breast Cancer Research Foundation. What I thought would be nothing but a bunch of guys wanting a date, turned out to be the complete opposite. So many people wanted to contribute to my cause.

The aroma of funnel cakes and fried food hung heavy in the air, a temptation too hard to resist since I only had a single muffin for breakfast. Cohen still hadn't arrived yet, but Miles stood off to the side with Jensen and Seth, animatedly talking about fishing. I was happy to see him getting along with my friends.

Everleigh elbowed me gently to get my attention. "Are you ready to break things off with Cohen?" she asked softly.

Dread filled my stomach at her question, and I nodded silently. "I am," I confessed, peering around at the crowd. "I keep waiting for him to show up."

Everleigh linked her arm with mine and rested her head on my shoulder. I never had a sister, but I always imagined it would be the kind of relationship I had with her.

"You'll be fine," she assured me. "It's as clear as day how much you and Miles belong with each other. How he looks at you reminds me of how Jensen looks at me."

That made me smile. "I remember saying something like that to you before you and Jensen got your heads out of your asses and decided to give each other a second chance."

Everleigh shook her head and laughed. "Exactly. Now I'm saying it to you." Her eyes widened and she gasped. "Oh, I forgot to tell you. A man and his wife came by here and paid for about a hundred tickets. They wanted to meet you and Miles, but you two were off grabbing a lemonade. I told them you'd be right back."

That piqued my interest. Each ticket was five dollars, so they just spent five hundred on a chance to spend two hours with me.

"Do you think it had to do with something about last night and the wreck?"

Everleigh shrugged. "Not sure, but they were really excited about meeting you."

Jensen and Miles came up to the table, and I couldn't stop my heart from skipping a beat every time Miles was near. He stopped in front of me and nodded toward the crowd.

"Jensen and I are going to walk around for a few. Do you want me to get you anything?"

I shook my head. "I'm good. Thanks."

Jensen leaned across the table and gave Everleigh a quick kiss. "Don't get into any trouble," he said to her.

Everleigh's mouth gaped in mock exasperation. "Who me? Never."

Miles winked at me and they walked off, stopping now and again to talk to various people.

Everleigh nudged me and pointed at the guys. "I think that's a bromance in the making. Jensen likes him."

My heart soared as I watched them until they disappeared through the crowd. "If you had told me a year ago that this was how my life would be, I never would've believed it."

Everleigh chuckled. "The world works in mysterious ways. I got a second chance with the man I have always loved, and now you're getting yours."

Two little girls with pigtails and smudged cheeks paused at the table, snickering as they grabbed two paper bags and took off.

"You know," Everleigh said, her eyes twinkling mischievously over at me. "If you and Miles get back together for good, you'll probably start a family soon, right?"

I laughed nervously, holding up a hand to pause her. "You are getting way ahead of yourself, my dear friend."

Everleigh shrugged an innocent shoulder. "Just saying. If you get pregnant soon, our kids will be so close in age they could be best friends."

My heart filled with warmth at the thought of a future with Miles and maybe even children of our own, but I quickly shook the idea out of my head when Everleigh's face froze and she gasped, her eyes locked on something across the way.

"Oh, my God."

My heart stopped. "What?"

I turned to see what she was looking at, and that was when I saw him. Dressed in a pair of khaki shorts and a light blue polo shirt with his dark hair perfectly coifed, Cohen had the biggest grin on his face when our eyes locked. My stomach swirled with nerves of dread, and it wasn't a good feeling. It was only a matter of time before Miles returned.

Were they going to be civil with each other? Or would they let their testosterone take over and act like cavemen? All I knew was that I wasn't looking forward to it.

"Hey, Cohen!" Everleigh shouted, waving a hand in the air.

He hurried over and leaned in to kiss me, but I was able to shift quickly so he kissed my cheek instead of my lips.

"You made it," I said, hating the guilt that weighed down on my chest.

Cohen was such an amazing man, and I was about to let him go, only I didn't want to tell him at the Spring Fling.

Cohen released a heavy sigh and ran a hand over his face. "I was beginning to think I wouldn't. Every time I tried to leave, something else would come up that needed to be handled." He peered around at all the people milling about. "There are a lot of people here."

"It's way more than we've ever had," Everleigh said. "The local businesses love it. All the tourists help keep them afloat."

Cohen smiled over at Everleigh. "That's good. I'm hoping Freddy reaches a point where he can buy back the surf shop from me." The only thing keeping Cohen in town *was* that surf shop.

"If he does buy it back," I wondered, "what does that mean for you? Isn't that the only reason why you moved here?"

Cohen's eyes flashed with need when he looked at me. "It was at first, but I have other reasons to stay." It would be so much easier if he had to move back to New York. Cohen nodded down at the ticket roll by Everleigh's hand. "So, how many guys have come by wanting a date with my girl?"

Everleigh chuckled nervously. "It's not just guys, Cohen. A lot of people want time with the town's hero." She draped an arm over my shoulder. "This lady helped save two people in a horrific car accident yesterday. It was on the news and everything."

Cohen's mouth gaped. "That's amazing, Nyla. I can't imagine what that's like."

I shrugged nonchalantly. "It's my job. Working as an ER doctor for all those years prepares you for stuff like that."

He pulled out his wallet and pointed at the roll of tickets on the table. "I'd like to buy three hundred tickets, please." I stared at him as if he'd lost his mind.

"That's fifteen hundred dollars, Cohen. You don't have to do that."

He smirked at me. "I know, but I want to. The more I buy, the more chances I'll win."

He gave Everleigh a wad of cash and she hid it with the rest of the money, while I gave him his copies of his tickets and put the rest in the box with all the others.

Cohen peered around at the crowd again and sighed. "So, is he here?" he asked, still looking at all the people.

A rock formed in my stomach; I knew he was going to ask. Everleigh glanced at me sheepishly and bit her lip.

When Cohen focused back on me, I nodded. "He is," I said, rubbing a hand over my aching chest. "I'm sure he'll be back in a minute."

Everleigh cleared her throat and nudged me. "Your minute is up. He's here now."

I followed her line of sight and time seemed to stand still as I waited for Miles to see Cohen standing by the table. When his eyes turned our way, it wasn't me that caught his attention first; his focus went straight to Cohen. His smile completely disappeared, and all that was written on his face was confusion . . . and anger. I didn't expect that strong of a reaction from him.

When I looked over at Cohen, he had the same look. The tension in the air was palpable, and it looked as if something was going on that I had no clue about.

Miles marched over to us with a determined stride, his eyes burning into Cohen's. "What the hell are you doing here?"

Cohen squared his shoulders and returned the hard gaze. "I could ask you the same question."

My heart paused in my chest as Jensen leaped between them. "All right, guys, let's take it down a notch."

Miles stepped back from Cohen, and I quickly moved out from behind the table to stand with them. Their eyes were locked on each other, almost like they'd done this dance before. But how did they know each other?

"What's going on?" I demanded.

Miles's jaw twitched, then he finally looked away and met my gaze. "Is this who you've been seeing?"

I glanced at Cohen and then back to him, giving an unsure nod. "Yes . . . why are you two acting as if you know each other?"

Cohen released an exasperated sigh. "It's because we do, Nyla."

Thick silence settled over us as I stared at both of them, anticipation pulsing through me for answers.

Finally, Miles pinned Cohen with a sharp look and gave his response—one I was not expecting.

"He's my cousin."

The world seemed to spin all around me and I stumbled back. Cousins? How was that even possible?

Miles reached out to steady me and so did Cohen, their hands clutching me in their grasps. By now, we'd garnered the attention of others around us, and the last thing I wanted was to cause a scene.

I pulled my arms away from them and held up my hands. "You guys need to do this somewhere else. Come with me."

My office was just two blocks away. I turned away from them and felt everything crashing all around me. Miles and Cohen were family.

Things just got way more complicated.

20

MILES

*T*he searing heat of anger burned through every cell in my body as I followed Cohen and Nyla down the street toward her office. How the hell was it possible that Cohen was the other guy in Nyla's life?

He was in love with her; it was clear as day.

Thinking of his hands on her brought out an unbridled rage within me. Cohen and I spent our entire childhood at odds with each other. Even though we were cousins, we looked nothing alike. His mother was my mom's sister and the one who married into the wealthy Sumner family. The Sumners had dark hair and green eyes, whereas my side were blond and blue.

Our families had been divided long before we were born, and with that came rivalries that had passed down to us. Cohen came from the wealthy side of the family, whereas mine struggled but had the love and respect of my grandparents.

No words were said as our footsteps echoed in the cool afternoon air. As we arrived at the office, Nyla pulled out her keys and opened the door, which closed behind us with a heavy thud.

Her expression was guarded, so I had no clue what she was thinking. One thing was for sure, I was ready to talk to Cohen. It couldn't have been a coincidence that he and Nyla just happened to run into each other. The guy was a sly bastard that would do anything to get what he wanted.

Nyla huffed and glanced back and forth between me and Cohen. "Look, I don't know what's going on here, but it's obvious you two need to talk it out." She pointed at the door. "I'm going to head back to the festival, and I don't want you two there if you can't be civil. I know this is a lot to take in." Cohen opened his mouth to speak, but Nyla cut him off with a hand in the air. "I don't think I'm ready to hear anything right now. I'm confused, and still trying to wrap my head around it." After a few minutes, her expression softened. "I'll talk to you both later, okay?" she said, glancing back and forth at us.

Instead of waiting for our replies, she bolted out the door. The second the door shut behind her, I faced off with Cohen.

"What are you doing in Oak Island?" I demanded.

Cohen sneered, a trait his side of the family had mastered over the years. "That's none of your business, but if you must know, I bought out Freddy's Surf Shop. They were going under and needed help."

I snorted with disbelief, narrowing my eyes at him. "Since when do you give a damn about small businesses?"

He crossed his arms over his chest, still wearing that smirk I loathed. "And since when do you care what I do?"

His words hung in the air between us like a challenge. "I don't. But when it comes to Nyla, I do. She's my wife, Cohen, and she's mine. I suggest you back off."

His smirk grew wider, and I wanted to punch it off his face. Nyla would have undoubtedly let him down delicately, but I wasn't about to. She didn't know him the way I did.

Cohen chuckled and looked at Nyla's picture on the wall beside Everleigh's. "She may be your *ex*-wife, but she's been mine for the past month." He leaned against the wall and shot me a triumphant grin. "I can give her everything you can't. She's been happy with me."

Nothing about him being in Oak Island made sense; he lived for the hustle and bustle of New York City, where women swooned over him everywhere he went. He loved the attention of the paparazzi; he always has.

"She doesn't want what you have to give," I snarled. "If you think she does, then you don't know her at all."

Cohen's lips curved into a smirk, and he ran his hands through his hair. "Believe it or not, she's changed me. I feel alive when I'm with her. I like who I am around her."

I rolled my eyes and laughed bitterly. "You're so full of shit. She hasn't even seen the real you yet."

His smirk evaporated, and his eyes ignited with fire as he stepped closer to me. "She has seen me . . . and I'm in love with her. That's why I'm not giving up on us without a fight."

I shook my head in disbelief. "She wants to be with me. Just go back to New York and spend your energy on someone else."

He gave a nonchalant shrug, then headed for the door. "If Nyla decides to be with you, that's fine by me. But make no mistake—I will still be a part of her life. You just have to get used to it."

With that, he walked out and left me standing there seething in anger. All these years, we had been competing against each other for our grandparents' attention, but this was different.

This time it was for Nyla's love and affection, and I knew Cohen wouldn't let go without a fight. No matter what happened, I had to stay on top of my game if I wanted any chance of winning.

21

NYLA

"*H*ow in the world does this even happen?" Everleigh asked. "The guy you're seeing is Miles's cousin? What are the odds of that?"

I scoffed. "Pretty good, apparently. I swear this is the kind of stuff you see in movies, not real life."

Everleigh chuckled and popped a Hershey's kiss into her mouth. "Exactly." She squeezed my arm reassuringly. "But what are you going to do?"

My heart was pounding like wild drumbeats inside my chest, but I kept a smile on my face as more people came by the table to enter the auction.

"I know what my heart wants," I said, keeping my voice low. "I just didn't think I would have a family rivalry to add to the mix."

I thought I was ready to talk to both guys, but I left them in my office. There was so much tension between them that you could cut it with a knife. When we were married, I remember Miles talking about a side of his family that he never got along with, but we never discussed it. I had never met them, not even at family gatherings. It was evident that Cohen was a part of that side.

Everleigh placed a soothing hand on my shoulder. "Try not to worry about everything right now. It's almost time for the auction draw and you need to look happy."

I lifted my brows at her. "You don't think I look happy? Am I exuding miserable vibes?"

She chuckled and shook her head. "No, you look great! Let's just hope your two men don't get upset if someone else wins you for the ice cream date."

Snorting, I tapped a finger against the auction box. "Cohen has three hundred chances in there. I don't even know how many Miles put in."

Her lips twitched in amusement as she looked away, but I could still see her smile.

"How many tickets did Miles buy?" I demanded.

Everleigh batted her long eyelashes before snatching another Hershey's kiss from the silver bowl on the table. She popped it into her mouth and snickered.

"Let's just say he's right up there with Cohen. So, basically, they both have a fair shot at winning."

A groan escaped my lips. "Great. Is it bad that I hope neither one of them win?"

Jensen walked up behind us and chuckled. "If it came down to a physical fight, Miles would win hands down."

I groaned again. "Hopefully, it doesn't come to that."

He snorted and wrapped his arm around Everleigh's shoulders. "If one of my cousins tried to get with Everleigh, you better believe I'd stop it."

Everleigh smacked a hand against his stomach. "Cohen didn't know. He and Miles were both shocked to see each other here."

Jensen shrugged and focused on me. "Either way, you're going to have your hands full."

My focus shifted toward the end of the street where my office was, and I watched as Cohen stormed out, his face a deep shade of crimson, with Miles not far behind him.

"Unfortunately, I believe you're right."

It was closing in on three o'clock, and an air of anticipation hung in the air as the crowd started to gather in the street. Gina and her husband waved at me while Autumn picked her way through the throng. She stood beside me wearing a bright pink Seaside Family Practice shirt that contrasted beautifully with her tanned skin and bright blonde hair.

"Did I miss anything?" she asked, taking her place beside me.

Jensen chuckled under his breath and kissed

Everleigh on the head before joining Seth, Trisha, Grady, and Michelle out in the crowd.

Autumn lifted her brows curiously. "What was that about?"

More people started to gather around, and I could see the mayor approaching; he was in his midfifties with salt and pepper hair, and was wearing a Hawaiian shirt and khaki pants.

I smiled at everyone gathered around and spoke through gritted teeth. "Take a look at everyone and tell me who you see," I said to her.

She raked her gaze through the crowd and her eyes lit up when she saw Miles, but they widened when she got over to Cohen.

"Oh, my God. They're both here. Have they met yet?"

Everleigh walked behind Autumn and leaned in close, her voice just above a whisper. "They're cousins."

Autumn's mouth dropped and she laughed. "Holy hell, this is exciting."

I rolled my eyes. "I'm so glad my love life amuses you."

The mayor, Stan Daley, finally reached us and shook our hands firmly. His blue eyes sparkled as he grinned widely at me.

"Are you ready for me to pick a winner?"

I resisted the urge to glance around at the crowd and kept my gaze on him as I nodded. "I am."

He cleared his throat and shifted in place, looking suddenly uncomfortable. "Just to warn you, my twenty-two-year-old son bought a ticket. If he wins, I'm sorry. I think he has a crush on you."

Autumn giggled. "So do a lot of other people, Mayor Daley. Dr. Clark is used to it." I glared at her, and it only made her giggle more. "Please don't fire me. I couldn't help it."

Everleigh patted Autumn's shoulder. "Don't worry. I won't let her."

"Yeah, yeah, yeah. Keep it up, you two," I grumbled under my breath.

They laughed even more, and despite myself, I felt the corners of my mouth twitch into a smile at their silliness, while my stomach knotted in anticipation. Stan held up his hands and waved at all the people gathered around.

"Hello, everyone!" he called out cheerfully. "Thank you so much for coming to our Spring Fling. This event is one of the biggest ones of the year in Oak Island and we're always so thankful to have the support."

As the mayor continued his speech, my mind drifted off to the possibility that the winner would most likely be either Miles or Cohen; they had the most chances inside the box. I wasn't ready to face them both yet.

When I took them to my office, I had no clue what to say to them. Usually, I never had a problem speaking my mind, but when I looked at them together, I panicked and had to leave. It didn't hit me until I got a good look at Cohen and Miles together. When I met Cohen for the first time at the restaurant, I remember thinking something seemed familiar about him; only I couldn't place it.

Now I knew why.

They were family. Even though their eye colors differed, they had the same shape and jaw structure.

"All right, folks," the mayor called out, "it's time to draw the winner! This lucky person will get an ice cream date with one of our beloved town doctors, Dr. Nyla Clark."

The crowd cheered and it made my heart slam harder in my chest. Stan reached into the box and swirled the tickets around. A few seconds later, he pulled out a small blue ticket.

"And the winner is . . ." he paused for dramatic effect.

My pulse beat so loudly in my ears that I couldn't even hear him as he shouted out the ticket number. Time seemed to slow down as everyone looked at their tickets to see if they had the winning numbers. But then I heard a shout and watched as the crowd separated as a man and woman came forward. They were older, probably in their early sixties. The man reminded me of my dad with combed-over white hair and glasses, and the woman had long, warm brown hair and honey-colored eyes. She looked exactly like someone I'd just met.

Everleigh clutched my arm. "That's the couple who wanted to meet you earlier. I'm so glad they won. They seem so sweet."

The woman waved at me, her smile so bright and genuine. Her husband handed Stan the ticket and he congratulated them. The crowd cheered and clapped, and when I looked over at Miles, he was clapping along with everyone and had a smile on his face. I knew he was happy that Cohen didn't win. However, when I glanced over in Cohen's direction, he was clearly angry by the tenseness in his jaw.

I joined Stan and the couple in front of the table.

"Dr. Clark," Stan said, beaming at the couple, "I'd like you to meet Dean and Joanne Rourke. Their daughter is Emily, the woman you helped save last night."

Joanne pulled me into an embrace, overcome with emotion. "Thank you so much for all you did," she cried. "I don't know if Emily would've survived if you and Miles weren't able to save Brian."

She let me go and wiped away her tears, only for more to fall. My eyes burned and I couldn't stop crying myself.

"I thought you looked familiar when you walked up. You and Emily have the same honey-colored eyes."

Joanne nodded and smiled. "I'm just glad she's still around for me to look at them."

Dean held out his hand and I shook it firmly. "Thank you for helping our baby girl and her husband. I told Emily that next time she needs to just hit the damn deer, instead of swerving off the road."

"That's what my dad said when I moved down here," I confessed. "There weren't any deer in downtown Boston when I lived there."

Joanne sighed. "If Brian's parents were alive, I know they'd be hearing pouring out their thanks as well." She frowned. "They passed away five years ago in a car accident."

A sharp pain thrummed in my chest. "That's horrible."

Joanne nodded. "We're all he has. I love that boy so much. He's so good to Emily." She took my hands in hers. "Will you please send our thanks to Miles? We owe him so much."

I smiled through my tears. "Why don't you tell him yourself."

I peered out at the crowd, and when my eyes locked on Miles, I waved for him to join us. However, I could feel Cohen's burning gaze on us in return.

When Miles closed the distance, I introduced him to Dean and Joanne and told him who they were. Joanne embraced him and started crying again, saying thank you repeatedly. Dean cleared his throat and wrapped his arm around Joanne's shoulders once she was done hugging Miles.

"I know this is an ice cream date with you," Dean said to me, but then he turned to Miles. "But is there any way for *you* to join us, too? Brian wouldn't be alive if it weren't for you."

Miles looked over at me for approval and I nodded. "I don't mind."

Miles grinned and Joanne linked her arm with his. "Great! We can walk to the ice cream shop together. I want to hear all about you."

Dean shook his head and laughed before turning to follow them. But before I could join them, I knew there was something else I had to do first. Miles looked back at me, and they all stopped and turned toward me.

"Give me one minute and we'll all go together," I said to them. "There's someone I need to speak to first."

Miles's smile faded slightly, especially when his gaze landed on something over my shoulder. I could feel Cohen's presence behind me.

Joanne beamed and pointed over at the sidewalk. "Go. We'll be right over there waiting on you."

I slowly turned around to face Cohen, my heart pounding when I noticed his rigid posture and the searing anger in his gaze as he glared at Miles. But when his eyes met mine, his expression softened.

"Why is Miles going with you?"

I stopped in front of him. "I doubt you saw the local news, but we saved two people in a car accident last night. The couple who won the auction are the parents of the girl I helped. Miles performed CPR on her husband and brought him back."

Cohen huffed, his voice taking on an icy sharpness. "Of course he did. He was always the golden boy of the family."

There was so much bitterness to his tone that it took me aback. Whatever was going on between them was deeply rooted.

Cohen hung his head and sighed. "I'm sorry. I shouldn't be like that. I'm glad Miles was able to save someone's life." His eyes met mine again and they were now filled with a multitude of unspoken questions. "We need to talk, Nyla. My mind is reeling right now. I'm sure there's a lot you want to know."

I snorted. "That's an understatement. But yes, we do need to talk."

His expression turned hopeful. "Can I stop by your place as soon as you're done at the ice cream shop?"

Miles wasn't going to like it, but I needed to sort everything out with Cohen.

"Sure," I said with a nod. "I'll text you when I'm on my way home." I reached out and squeezed his hands, my heart aching at the thought of hurting him. "See you in a little bit."

Turning on my heel, I returned to Miles, Dean, and Joanne, and we walked up the street to the ice cream shop. Dean and Joanne walked inside, but Miles stepped in my way before I could follow them.

"What's going on?" he asked, his voice was tight and his gaze searched mine.

I tipped my head back and exhaled slowly. "You're not going to like it, but Cohen wants to see me after this date. You know I need to talk to him."

His jaw clenched, the muscle twitching beneath his skin. "He's not a good guy, Nyla. The man can manipulate anyone; you can't trust anything he says or does."

"I can't begin to understand why you feel that way. I want to know everything about your—and his —past. Believe me, I'm super curious to hear both of your sides." I took his hands in mine. "But Cohen has never given me a reason not to trust him. All I'm going to do is talk to him."

Miles sighed heavily and pulled me into his arms. "Can I be there with you?"

I laughed lightly and shook my head. "That'll only make things more awkward."

He let me go, his blue eyes piercing into mine. "Then will you come to see me after you're done with him?"

A smile spread across my face. "Yes."

22

NYLA

*B*y the time we were done at the ice cream shop, the festival was over, and most of the tents and vendors were gone. The orange cones had been removed so the city could open the road again.

I had to remind myself to call Everleigh and Jensen and thank them for packing our stuff. I planned on helping once the ice cream date with Dean and Joanne ended, but it ran an hour over. It turned out that it wasn't just them, me, and Miles. Joanne had video called Emily, who was in Brian's hospital room. Miles and I were able to talk to them; it was heartwarming. It turned out that Emily was pregnant and that the baby was doing great. Brian and Emily said that if it were a girl, they would name her Nyla; if it were a boy, it would be Miles.

I was floating on air when Miles and I left the ice

cream shop. He walked me to my office, where I'd left my car the day before. He was hesitant about Cohen coming to my house, but he promised not to show up.

Once in my car, I pulled out my phone and texted Cohen.

> Me: I'm on my way to the house. Meet me there in 10?

A few seconds later, Cohen's reply came in.

> Cohen: I'll be there.

A flash of silver glinted from the driveway as I pulled down my street. Cohen had arrived before me, and was leaning against his silver Bentley with his arms crossed in front of him.

When I parked beside him, he came over to open my car door. "How did everything go?" he asked.

I couldn't hold back my smile. "It was great," I said, getting out of my car. "I got to see Emily and Brian through video. They're doing great *and* they're expecting a baby."

Cohen smiled and shut my car door. "That's pretty awesome. I'm glad you got to see them."

We stood in awkward silence for a few seconds while I tried to find the right words to say.

Cohen nodded toward the back of the house. "Do you want to talk on your deck? It feels nice outside."

I walked over to my passenger's side and grabbed my purse from the front seat. "Sure. Why don't you go back there while I take my stuff inside."

Cohen nodded and disappeared around the side of the house while I went in and set my purse on the counter. I watched him sit down in one of the Adirondack chairs and gaze out at the channel. We had sat out there many times the past month, but now I felt a strange distance between us. The emotions that used to swirl around me when he was nearby were absent now. I think I'd always known that no one could ever measure up to Miles and fill the void he left in my heart.

Taking a deep breath, I slowly stepped outside onto the patio. Cohen flashed me an uneasy smile, his green eyes searching my face for an answer as he leaned forward and rested his elbows on his knees.

"Let's just cut to the chase, Nyla," he said quietly. "You don't have to sugarcoat anything for me. Just tell me what you want."

I hesitated for a split second before responding. "I can tell you what I don't want," I said softly. "I don't want to hurt you."

He snorted once and dropped his gaze back to the water. "You're choosing Miles, aren't you?"

"I am," I answered.

His jaw tensed as he considered my words, and he ran his thumb over the back of his hand, probably trying to control his emotions. He then looked up at me and asked a question that made my chest tighten.

"Did you care about me at all?"

I leaned forward so that our faces were closer together, wanting him to meet my gaze. When he did, I stared right into his eyes.

"Of course I did. I still do. But you being related to Miles makes things a little more complicated." I leaned forward to get closer to him, hoping he'd look at me. When he did, I stared right into his eyes. "How did you not know I was married to your cousin? Surely, you would've heard about our wedding when it happened. My name isn't exactly common."

Miles's words of not trusting Cohen rang in my head, which was why I wanted to ask the questions.

Cohen shook his head and laughed. "I wasn't invited to the wedding, Nyla. Nobody on my side of the family was." He shrugged as if it didn't bother him. "Honestly, I doubt I would've gone even if I had been invited."

"What happened between you two?" I asked, wondering what could've been so bad that Miles and Cohen hated each other the way they did.

Cohen's jaw tensed as he threw his arms up and shook his head. He spoke slowly as if stifling a deep rage.

"Guess it was a combination of things. Our grandfather always favored Miles over me, no matter what I did. He hated my father, so I guess his loathing passed down to me." He scoffed. "My dad was able to give my mother everything she wanted. You would've thought that'd make my grandfather happy." He clenched his fists tightly and turned away from me. "My grandparents paid for Miles to play sports and go off to summer camps, while I had to help my dad with the family business. I hated it when I'd see my grandparents light up when Miles came into the room. As I got older, I grew to resent him." His gaze met mine again and his face darkened with an almost tangible anger. "I resented all of them. There's been bad blood ever since."

A heavy silence fell between us and my heart hurt for him, but I have never been more sure of what I wanted. Cohen's body relaxed and I could feel the anger dissipate from around him.

"Where do we go from here?" I asked him.

He sat back in his chair and gazed out at the water. "That depends. Do I have a fighting chance or is your heart made up?"

It killed me having to break his heart. I shook my head and reached over to take his hand.

"I'm sorry, Cohen. I don't want to make things more difficult between you and Miles, but I have so much history with him. Miles has always had my heart."

Cohen looked down at our clasped hands and

sighed. "I guess there's nothing else I can do." He grabbed my other hand and helped me up, pulling me closer to him. "If this is going to be the end of us, let me take you out to dinner one last time. Tomorrow night, just me and you. Then, afterward, I don't see any other option but to take a plane back to New York."

My stomach clenched. The last thing I wanted to do was to run him out of town.

"Would you be leaving for good?"

He shrugged. "There wouldn't be any other reason for me to stay."

"What about the surf shop?"

"They don't physically need me here, Nyla. I can do what I have to do for them anywhere in the world." He stepped closer, his eyes searching mine. "One more dinner. That's all I ask. All you need to do is say yes." Cohen picked up on my hesitation and squeezed my hands reassuringly. "We're friends, aren't we?"

"Of course," I replied, but I knew Miles would hate the idea of me going to dinner with him.

Cohen let my hands go and stepped back. "Miles will be okay. I mean, hell, he has you now. He can deal with a couple of hours without you so you can have dinner with me."

Which was true; it would only be for a short while. I owed Cohen that.

"Okay," I gave in. "Dinner tomorrow."

Cohen smiled triumphantly, his face lighting up with joy. "Great. I'll pick you up at five o'clock."

He started to walk off, but then I called after him. "Hey, where are we going? I need to know what to wear!"

He turned around to face me and smiled. "It's a surprise." His eyes roamed down my body and he smiled mischievously. "And wear whatever you want. I know you don't care for the fancy stuff."

He disappeared around the side of the house, and I listened to his engine rev. Once I knew he was gone, I grabbed my phone out of my pocket and texted Miles.

> Me: It's done. I'm headed over to your place.

By the time I walked inside, he messaged back.

> Miles: That was fast. What do you want to do tonight?

A smile spread across my face as so many thoughts filtered through my mind.

> Me: I'm sure we'll figure something out.

*E*ven though it pained my heart to hurt Cohen, it also freed me. Nothing could hold me back from Miles now; I could be with him in every way possible without feeling guilty.

There was so much excitement coursing through my veins that I could barely keep my hands steady on the steering wheel. As I pulled up to Miles's beach house rental, I could feel the butterflies in my stomach fluttering faster and faster. The anticipation of finally being with him was palpable, and all my senses were heightened.

I parked my car in the driveway and breathed deeply to try and calm myself down. But as soon as I got out of the vehicle, Miles was waiting for me at the top of the stairs, shirtless and wearing only a pair of khaki shorts.

My heart skipped a beat at the sight of him.

He smiled and I couldn't help but stare at him for a few moments. All I could think about was how I couldn't wait to feel his rough hands on my skin, smell the scent of his cologne, and hear his voice as he whispered in my ear.

"Hey there, sunshine," he said as he descended the stairs, his outstretched hand eagerly reaching for mine.

As soon as our fingers twined together, I was hit with an electric wave that shot up my arm and spread throughout my body.

Grabbing my hand more firmly, he pulled me up the rest of the stairs and folded me into his embrace. His gaze afire, full of emotion, made me tremble from head to toe.

"You're mine again. How does that feel?"

I slipped my arms around his neck and moved closer until our lips almost touched. "It feels great," I murmured softly against his mouth.

His smirk showed me what he had in mind for us; it matched what I wanted, too.

"What do you want to do?" he asked, his voice low and husky.

I moved my gaze to his lips and then back to his eyes. "I don't want to waste any more time."

The sound of waves crashing against the shore only heightened the anticipation between us. Miles leaned in for a kiss, and I melted into his embrace.

His lips felt like sweet nectar on mine, and I was lost in the moment, consumed by my desire for him.

We moved inside, and Miles pulled me into the bedroom. The room was dimly lit, but some sunlight shone through the window. He kissed me passionately, and I could feel his warmth enveloping me.

Miles lifted me up and gently placed me on the bed. He looked down at me, his eyes so full of emotion that I could feel the burn behind mine.

"I love you so much, Nyla. I keep thinking this is a dream."

I cupped his cheeks and rubbed my thumb over his lips. "Oh, no. This is real. And I'm going to enjoy every minute of it."

He chuckled lightly and kissed me again. "So am I."

Being with Miles again for the first time in all these years was even more passionate than before; it was exhilarating. Nothing was holding us back. It was just me and him and our love for each other.

"I'm assuming you're staying here tonight?" Miles asked, grinning at me from the couch as I walked into the living room dressed in one of his T-shirts and sweatpants.

Laughing softly, I sat down beside him. "Is that okay?"

Miles pulled me into his arms, his legs wrapping around mine. "I want us together every night. There's no reason for us to be apart again."

The thought of that made my heart soar with happiness, but there was still something I had to tell him and I dreaded it. A sheepish sigh escaped my lips when I sat up and faced him.

"There's something I need to tell you."

His smile faded slightly and he let out a small huff. "Let me guess, it's about Cohen." When I nodded, he sat up and waved for me to continue. "I knew we were going to have to talk about your conversation with him at some point." His hungered gaze raked down my body. "Although, I did enjoy the distraction earlier."

I bit my lip and smiled. "I did, too. We still have the rest of the night to enjoy more."

Miles chuckled and shook his head. "All right, tell me about my cocksucker of a cousin so we can get this over with."

I didn't want to delay the inevitable, so I just blurted it out. "Cohen wants to take me out to one last dinner tomorrow before he goes back to New York," I said quickly.

Miles's expression of ease quickly changed to anger. "Seriously? What the hell is he trying to do? He's up to something."

I blew out a sigh. "He's not trying to do anything, Miles. It's just one last dinner before he leaves town."

He scoffed. "Did he actually say he was leaving?"

I nodded and clutched his hands reassuringly. "Yes. Which is good for us. We don't have to worry about seeing him around town."

Miles leaned his head back on the couch and groaned. "I know I can't tell you not to go, but I'm not happy about this." He turned his head to look at me again. "But I trust you. I'm just ready for that asshole to pack up and go back to New York." His gaze narrowed slightly. "What did he tell you about our family?"

I shrugged. "Not much. I know there's a lot of jealousy he has toward you."

Miles growled in disgust. "That's an understatement. You wouldn't believe all the shit he did to me when we were young."

I pressed a finger to his lips. "I don't want to spend this amazing evening talking about Cohen. This is *our* night. I want to concentrate on us and where we go from here."

Miles pulled me down so I was lying on top of his chest and wrapped me in his arms. "I can live with that." He kissed the top of my head. "I start teaching classes this coming Monday. I'm going to see if any of the stations are hiring."

Excitement bubbled throughout my body and I

turned his arms, resting my chest against his. "Are you really going to move here? Like now?"

He smiled mischievously. "I don't see why not. Didn't you say earlier, before we had our fun in the bedroom, that you didn't want to waste any more time?"

I laughed. "Yeah."

He shrugged. "Well, all right, then. I have so much to do. I have to sell my house in Virginia and find a place out here."

His eyes twinkled and I smacked his chest. "Stop being ridiculous. You can move into my house; I might have a spare bedroom."

He poked his fingers at my sides, tickling me. I squealed and tried to push him off, but he picked me up in his arms and tossed me on the couch, his body pressing me into the cushions.

"Spare bedroom, huh? I see how you want it to be," he teased.

I rolled my eyes. "You know I'm kidding."

Wrapping my arms around his neck, I drew him in closer to kiss him. "We're going to do things right this time. I know what's important." My eyes burned and I let the tears fall so he could see how much he meant to me. "I'm never going to let you down again," I promised.

Miles shook his head. "I don't care about the past anymore. I'm only looking toward the future." He kissed my cheek and down my neck. "It'll be better this time. I promise."

My heart filled with so much joy it almost felt like it was too much to contain. "I promise, too," I whispered.

24

MILES

There were so many things I wanted to tell Nyla about Cohen, but I held back. Telling her would only make it look like I was trying to turn her against him. He wasn't the type of man to be trusted. I always considered myself a good judge of character, and he was far from a good person.

Cohen and I grew up together, and he did everything he could to make my life miserable. His parents bought him everything and he boasted every chance he got. When my parents bought me something new, Cohen would destroy it. It was like a game to him.

Did my grandparents show me more attention? Yes, they did, but that wasn't my fault.

They knew I didn't have much and tried to make my childhood as memorable as possible. I loved fishing with my grandfather and helping my grandmother in her gardens. Cohen was always above all that and made it known that he had no interest in getting his hands dirty.

However, a part of me always wondered what Cohen would be like if he didn't have a self-absorbed douchebag for a father. My uncle wasn't the type to do manual labor. He had the money to pay for everything to get done for him. Even my aunt—who I had adored as a kid—changed into someone I probably wouldn't recognize if I saw her today. Literally.

She had walked past me at the last family reunion many years ago, and I had to do a double take. The number of plastic surgeries she's had has completely changed her appearance. That was the last time my mom had seen her sister.

Sadly, the family soon became nonexistent once my grandparents passed away. They were what held the family together. With them gone, that was it. The only time I ever saw Cohen after that was in the tabloids. Maybe he was different with Nyla, but I doubted it; he was still the same conniving piece of shit I'd known my entire life. He could fool anyone into thinking he was a decent person. That was exactly how his father was. Because of him, my mom never spoke to her sister anymore.

Cohen and his father were master manipulators.

I hated the thought of Nyla going to dinner with

him, but it was only for a couple of hours. After tonight, never again.

I walked through the beach house one last time to make sure I hadn't left anything.

"Everything look good?" Nyla called out from the living room.

After looking around the bedroom and bathroom, I shut off the lights. "I think so!" I shouted, grabbing my bag off the bed.

Things were moving a lot faster than I thought they would. However, I wasn't going to complain. Nyla and I talked the entire night, and she said it was a waste of money for me to continue renting a vacation house when I could just stay with her.

For the next two weeks, while I worked in the area, we were going to be living together. Afterward, I would run to Virginia and get everything ready to sell my house along with putting in my notice at the station.

Our future was finally coming together.

I joined Nyla in the living room and couldn't get over how beautiful she was. She was wearing a pair of jeans and a light purple sleeveless top that hugged her curves perfectly. Her red hair hung down in waves down her back, and her majestic blue eyes were so clear they could be seen from far away.

In a little less than an hour, she would be with Cohen.

I tried getting her to wear my T-shirt and

sweatpants from last night, but she refused. I kept hoping time would slow down and five o'clock would never come. Luckily, with me staying at Nyla's house, I would be there when he picked her up and when he dropped her off.

Did I want to gloat about it in front of him? Of course, but I wasn't going to.

Nyla and I walked out of the beach house and I locked the doors, securing the key in the box by the front door.

"Now that you're going to be living at my house, you can cut the grass," Nyla said, winking at me over her shoulder.

I would do anything she asked of me. She stopped by her Jeep and I went to my 4Runner, tossing my bag in the back seat.

"Does that mean you'll be cooking every night?" I asked, laughing. "Or are we getting takeout like we used to?"

She snorted. "Definitely, not. I don't see how we did that all the time. I love cooking now." Her eyes widened and she gasped. "But on Tuesdays, eating at The Beachcomber is a tradition. You've already met Jensen and Seth, but you'll get to meet Seth's wife, my friend Michelle, and her husband."

Oak Island was already starting to feel like home.

"I can't wait," I said.

We both got into our vehicles and headed to Nyla's house. When we arrived, she cleaned a few drawers in her dresser and helped me unpack my things into them. It was all becoming a reality.

Nyla grabbed my toiletry bag and set my toothbrush in the holder beside hers. I came up behind her and wrapped my arms around her waist. She stared at our reflection in the mirror and smiled.

"I know we spent some years apart, but with you here now, it almost feels like no time has passed." Her smile faded. "Although that time apart was the worst moment of my life. Now it seems as if it was all just a bad dream."

I nodded in agreement. "I know how you feel. It was hard to be happy about anything."

Nyla's phone beeped and I groaned. Sliding my arms away from her, I stepped back so she could grab her phone out of her back pocket.

Her eyes met mine in the mirror as soon as she finished reading the text. "It's him," she whispered. "He's on his way to pick me up."

I clenched my fists and tried to ignore the tightness in my chest. Huffing, I walked out of the bathroom. "Of course he is."

She followed me down the hall and past the living room to the kitchen. "What are you going to do, Miles?"

Spinning around, I flashed her a halfhearted smile. "I'm going to stand with you while you wait on him."

After opening the kitchen door, I gestured for

her to walk out with me. Nyla stepped forward and pressed her body against mine, encircling my neck with her soft arms.

"You have nothing to worry about."

I didn't doubt her feelings for me, but there was still that sense of insecurity at the back of my mind.

"I know," I said, holding her closer. I pressed my forehead to hers and breathed in her strawberry scent. "It's just I know Cohen can give you anything you want. Most women would jump at the chance for something like that."

She snorted and clutched my face in her hands, her blue eyes never leaving mine. "I'm not like most women and you know that. I prefer pizza and pajamas on the weekend, not fancy dinner parties and multi-thousand-dollar dresses."

She stepped away and lifted her brows, waiting for my acknowledgment. I nodded and kissed her again.

"I know. I'm just ready for you to get this pity party dinner over with. Cohen doesn't deserve this time with you."

I hated the fact that she felt she owed him dinner. Nyla was a strong and intelligent woman, but Cohen could manipulate anyone. If he tried anything with Nyla, I was going to make sure the paparazzi wouldn't recognize him when he returned to New York.

A few seconds later, the sound of Cohen's sports

car rumbled just down the street before he pulled into the drive, arrogantly smiling at me from beneath his aviators.

Nyla stepped in front of me, blocking my view of him. "I'll be back soon. Do you have any plans for tonight?"

I shrugged noncommittally. "I might grab some dinner from The Beachcomber."

She smiled and nodded. "Sounds good. I'll see you soon."

Cohen came up behind her and glared at me, but his eyes softened when she turned to face him. *Smug bastard.*

"Are you ready?" he asked her.

She glanced at me again and smiled before walking with him to his car. It took all I had not to tell Cohen to leave and just lift Nyla over my shoulder and take her inside. But I couldn't do that without pissing Nyla off.

Cohen opened the passenger's side door for Nyla and shut it once she got inside. Instead of getting in to join her, he walked over to me.

"It's mighty nice of you to let Nyla be with me tonight."

My jaw clenched so hard I thought my teeth would break. "She's coming home to me. That's all I care about."

Cohen smirked. "You never know, she could change her mind."

Anger coursed through my veins, and I stepped toward him. "If you try anything with her tonight, I'll break every bone in your face."

Cohen chuckled and walked backward toward the car. "I'd like to see you try."

That smirk still lingered on his face as he got into the car beside Nyla and drove away. All I could do was watch until the car disappeared around the corner, wishing I would've just punched him like I wanted to.

"What was that all about?" I asked.

It was clear whatever Cohen had said made Miles mad.

The engine purred softly as Cohen pulled out onto the main road, his gaze never leaving the asphalt. Finally, he shrugged, his features etched with a hint of amusement.

"He's not happy you're going out with me tonight. Surely, you're not surprised by that."

His deep laugh made my stomach clench, and I couldn't help but feel guilty. I wouldn't be too pleased if the situation was reversed and Miles was going out with an ex-girlfriend.

"No. I know he's not happy."

Staring out at the passing landscape, I noticed we'd left the ocean view behind and were heading inland. The car smelled like Cohen's cologne, a heady mix of sandalwood and musk; it was utterly different from Miles's scent, which was crisp and cool like peppermint.

"Where are we going?" I wondered.

Cohen's grin widened and we turned down a long tree-lined road. I couldn't see anything beyond the trees.

"You're about to find out," he said, his face full of excitement.

My breath caught once we rounded the bend in the road and I saw what awaited us; a private airfield with a sleek white jet parked on the runway.

Cohen pulled up to the small airstrip and parked his car.

"You ready?"

I turned to him and lifted my brows. "You never said anything about flying anywhere."

Laughing, Cohen waved a hand dismissively in the air. "We're not going far. Driving would take about five hours, but we can fly there in one." He placed a hand reassuringly over mine. "It'll be fun. You'll like where we're going."

He stepped out, took off his sunglasses, and walked over to the jet, where the pilot waited by the steps leading into the plane.

I pulled out my phone and sent a quick text to Miles.

Me: Looks like I'll be home a little later than I thought.

Cohen turned to me and waved for me to join him.

"The jet's ready!" he called out.

I was hoping Miles would text before I got on the jet, but as soon as Cohen and I were inside, the engines hummed.

Soon enough, the plane was soaring through the air, its engines roaring like an animal in flight. As we zoomed past thick clouds and away from the city lights, my cell phone signal faded into nothingness.

26

MILES

*A*fter seeing Nyla's text, my chest tightened with fury. I had no clue what she meant, but I knew it involved Cohen's scheming.

I tried to call and text her back, yet received no response.

As the minutes dragged on and my anxiety swelled, I decided to grab the takeout order from The Beachcomber that I had placed earlier. The parking lot was filled with cars and the sky was darkening ominously with thick clouds promising a storm.

When I opened my car door and placed the to-go bag onto the passenger seat, I felt a gentle tap on my shoulder. Startled, I whirled around to find a young woman with long blonde hair standing behind me.

She appeared frazzled and desperate as she chewed her bottom lip nervously. "I apologize for bothering you," she began haltingly, "but my car has a flat tire, and it looks like it's about to start storming any minute now. I don't want to be stuck in this parking lot with no one to help me once it starts."

There was something familiar about the woman, but I couldn't place her.

"Have we met before?" I asked her.

She shook her head and shrugged. "I don't see how. I'm pretty sure I would've remembered you if we did."

Her tone had turned flirty, but I just stared at her in response. She cleared her throat and nodded toward the road.

"I just got to Oak Island this morning. I'm staying at the Sandy Shore Bed & Breakfast. I thought it was time for a *solo* vacation." Her eyes twinkled when she said that, and it was clear she'd said it that way for a reason. "My name's Candace Parks," she said, holding out her hand.

Groaning inwardly, I shook her hand firmly, then let go. "Miles Henley. Which car is yours?" I asked, peering around the parking lot.

My plan was to help her and leave.

Candace pointed toward the other side of the parking lot where a bright red Mazda Miata sat.

"It's the back left tire," she informed me.

We walked over and her arm brushed up against

mine several times. I tried putting some distance between us, but she kept getting closer.

"Do you have a spare in the trunk?" I questioned.

She nodded and opened her trunk. Luckily, I had changed numerous tires over the years, so I knew it wouldn't take long.

As I worked on changing the tire, Candace continued to make small talk, asking me about my line of work and if I was from around the area. I tried to keep my answers short but couldn't ignore how her eyes sparkled with interest.

Something about her didn't sit right with me. It was like there was a hidden agenda behind her flirty behavior, especially with the way she kept trying to touch me. What really gave me déjà vu was that this had happened to me once before with a woman who looked exactly like Candace Parks, only it was many years ago.

I had always prided myself on being a good judge of character, and I could tell something was off with the woman.

Once I finished changing the tire, I wiped my hands on my jeans and checked my phone. There was still nothing from Nyla.

Candace moved closer, her fingers gliding up my chest. "How do you want me to pay you for fixing my tire?"

I backed up and moved her hand away. "I'm not

interested in that," I said, my tone clipped. "I'm with someone."

She gave me a mock frown and continued to touch me. "That hasn't stopped others before. I have no doubt I can give you a night you'll never forget."

Suddenly, in one quick move, she flung her arms around my neck and pressed her lips to mine.

I pushed her away quickly and held up my hands. "What the hell is wrong with you?"

Without missing a beat, I turned on my heel and headed straight for my car, my gut clenching with frustration.

"If you change your mind, you know where to find me!" she shouted.

Huffing, I jumped in my car and sped away as fast as possible. The night wasn't off to a good start, and I had a feeling it was only going to get worse.

*W*e landed at a private airfield in the mountains of North Carolina and there was a black limo waiting for us on the strip. The air was much cooler and crisp than at the coast.

Everleigh told me many times about how gorgeous the Great Smoky Mountains were, and she didn't lie. It was breathtaking riding around the winding roads and seeing the vast expanse of the mountain range in the distance.

"We're almost there," Cohen said, grinning at me.

I glanced down at my jeans and top. "Hopefully I'm dressed okay for wherever we're going. This place must be fantastic for you to want to hop on a jet and come here on a whim."

Cohen chuckled and shrugged nonchalantly. "You'll see. It's a surprise."

About twenty minutes later, the driver took us

down a single-lane road surrounded by thick forest. The sun wasn't far from setting, but slivers of deep orange peeked through the trees.

Soon, we pulled up to a luxurious cabin, lights twinkling from inside the various rooms.

"What is this place?" I asked, taking it all in.

It didn't look like a restaurant.

Cohen stepped out of the limo and extended a hand to me. I took it and he helped me out, flourishing a hand at the opulence before us.

"This is one of my homes. We're eating dinner here."

My mouth dropped. "One of your homes? When did that happen?"

Cohen let my hand go and beamed at the cabin with pride. "I bought it a couple of weeks ago. I was going to bring you here for a vacation." His smile faded when he looked at me. "Then everything with Miles happened. But I knew I wanted you to see this place; that's why I had our dinner catered in." His smile came back, and he held out his arm. "Shall we?"

I linked my arm around his and clutched my purse in my other arm as we walked up the steps to the sparkling glass front door. Cohen opened it and everything inside was nothing but pure elegance and charm. The grand entrance led us into a beautifully decorated living room with a large fireplace and antique furnishings. The scent of a delicious meal wafted through the air, and my stomach growled in response.

Cohen led me to the dining room, where a table was set for two, complete with crystal glasses, silver cutlery, and candles flickering in the dim light. There were several different covered dishes on the table, but I could smell the fragrant aromas coming from them. As we took our seats, Cohen poured us each a glass of red wine, clinking his against mine.

"To us," he said, his eyes sparkling with an intensity that sent shivers down my spine. It would be much easier if he didn't look at me like that.

I brought the wine to my lips, taking only a tiny sip. It was clear that Cohen had other things on his mind besides an innocent meal between friends. He uncovered the dishes and smiled.

"I hope you're hungry."

There was salad, soup, roasted chicken with herb butter, garlic mashed potatoes, and steamed asparagus. We ate silently for a few moments, and I savored every bite of the perfectly cooked meal. I welcomed the silence, but it wasn't long before Cohen broke it.

"There's something I want to show you," he said, standing and offering me his hand.

I took it and he led me outside and down the deck stairs, where twinkling lights lit up a small pavilion nestled into a garden with colorful flowers.

The second I stepped into the gazebo, I felt a rush of anxiety swarm through me.

Soft music played in the background and dozens of candles flickered around us, their light casting strange shadows on the lacy curtains that hung from the sides. When I turned to Cohen, he was already kneeling before me, a magnificent diamond ring held between his fingers.

My mouth dropped open in shock and my breath caught in my throat as I watched him slide it onto my finger. It felt surreal as if I had stepped into an alternate reality — did he really just propose to me? His grip was tight as he brought me closer, and his dark eyes burned fiercely.

"Nyla, I thought I could handle you choosing Miles over me," he said, "but I can't. I'm in love with you and I want to marry you." He gestured to his cabin behind us, with its sprawling grounds and luxurious architecture. "Look what I can give you. Anything you want can be yours. I would do anything to make you happy."

I could feel his eyes boring into me, willing me to say yes. He failed to understand that having expensive things wasn't what I wanted. I didn't want a grand life in the public eye. Cohen was a fighter, and I could see in his eyes that he didn't want to give up on me, but I didn't love him as I did Miles.

Reaching up, I cupped his face with my hands, letting the diamond ring on my finger reflect the flickering flames from the candles around us. It had to be worth tens of thousands of dollars, but that meant nothing to me; it was the most expensive thing I would ever have on my body.

Cohen stared at me expectantly, and it broke my heart knowing that what I was about to say would hurt him.

"I'm so sorry, Cohen. I made my choice." I slowly stepped back, and his eyes darkened.

"How is this possible? I don't see how you can choose Miles over me."

Sadly, I lifted my shoulders in a shrug. "I love him, Cohen. I married him."

He growled. "But it didn't work. What we have is real, Nyla." He averted his gaze and huffed before meeting my eyes again. "Do you not love me?"

Tears burned behind my eyes, but I stood firm. "I care about you deeply, and we had an amazing month together. But . . ." I paused and took a deep breath. "But I'm not *in* love with you." Swallowing hard, I slid the ring off my finger and held it out to him. "You'll find the right woman one day. It's just not me." He made no move to take the ring, so I reached for his hand and gently set it in his palm. "I think it's time you take me home."

Turning on my heel, I walked up the steps toward the cabin's back porch and went inside. There was still a little wine in my glass, so I finished it off. I needed a lot more where that came from, but I was going to wait until I got home to Miles. He was going to need the alcohol when I explained everything that had happened.

I sat at the table for a few minutes while waiting for Cohen to enter. Luckily, it didn't take him long, but the tension in the air was palpable. He had his phone pressed to his ear, but he huffed in annoyance when a disconnected beep echoed from the other end.

"Dammit," he hissed, closing his eyes and pinching the bridge of his nose.

"What's wrong," I asked, feeling a sense of dread take over my stomach.

He nodded at my purse that was under the table. "Do you mind seeing if you can call anyone? I don't have service."

That wasn't good.

Reaching into my purse, I pulled out my phone, thinking there would be a message from Miles, but there was nothing. My phone had no cell service. Still, I tried to dial Miles's number, but all I got was that incessant beeping I had heard from Cohen's a few minutes prior.

"I got nothing," I said, setting my phone on the table. The time was ticking by, and I really wanted to get back on the plane to head home. "When is your driver supposed to pick us up?" I asked.

Cohen paced the floor and tried making another call, only for the same beeping to echo across the room. "That's who I'm trying to call." He focused on me. "If I can't get in touch with him, he won't know to pick us up."

It felt as if my stomach had plummeted to my feet.

"That means we have no way out of here," I snapped.

I could only imagine what Miles would think if I didn't make it home. Cohen ran a hand through his hair and sat at the kitchen table with me.

"Richard knows that if I don't call him tonight, he's to be here by six in the morning. I know you have patients scheduled, and I wanted to make sure you were back in time for work."

His words made my blood boil and I stood, my chair scraping against the hardwood floor. "If you don't call him tonight?" I spat, feeling the anger well in my chest. "Whatever made you think I'd want to spend the night here with you?"

All he did was stare at me with his penetrating green gaze. "Oh, I don't know, Nyla," he replied with a shrug of his shoulders as he got to his feet. "I thought maybe you'd accept my proposal."

And then afterward, we'd spend the night together.

Miles was right. Cohen did have something up his sleeve tonight.

Grabbing my purse from under the table, I quickly zipped it and stormed for the door.

"Where are you going?" Cohen demanded, following a few paces behind me.

"I'm walking down the road until I get a phone signal," I snarled. "If I don't get home tonight, it will make Miles think the worst." When I got to the door, I stopped and glared back at him. "I'm assuming that's what you wanted in the first place."

Cohen held up his hands in surrender, but his voice was tinged with worry. "Nyla, I'm sorry for whatever you think I've done. Honestly, I thought there was a chance I could change your mind."

But no matter how much he pleaded, my mind was made up; this dinner had been a mistake.

With a heavy sigh, I opened the door and peered into the darkness outside. We were in the middle of nowhere in the North Carolina mountains, and walking down winding roads alone wasn't an option. Not to mention there were probably bears and other animals running around.

Huffing in frustration, I slammed the door shut and shifted my attention to the opulent staircase leading to the second level of the cabin.

"If I'm stuck here for the night," I said with clenched teeth, "I'm going to need a room. Which one can I take?"

Cohen shrugged, his face a mask of guarded emotion. "Any of them. I'll stay down here and keep trying to make calls. If anything changes, I'll let you know."

Without another word, I went up the stairs and randomly picked a room. When I opened the door, I didn't even turn on the lights to see what everything looked like. I lay on the bed and closed my eyes, my stomach churning with worry. I could only imagine the kinds of things that were going to go through Miles's mind.

28

MILES

$\mathcal{M}$idnight had rolled around and there was still no word from Nyla. All I'd gotten from her was that last text saying she would be home later than she thought. I didn't know if she was okay or if something was wrong. Not knowing drove me insane. Every time I tried calling her, it would go straight to voice mail.

I'd paced the living room floor for the past two hours, my mind going to places it shouldn't. I didn't want to think of Nyla with Cohen and what was happening between them. I trusted Nyla with every fiber of my being, but Cohen? The man was a snake in the grass, always slithering around, trying to get what he wanted.

As I sat on the couch, my anxiety skyrocketing, my phone finally rang. My heart raced as I reached over to get it off the coffee table. I hoped to see

Nyla's name on the screen, but that wasn't what greeted me.

Instead, it said *Restricted Caller*.

I accepted the call and quickly put the phone to my ear. "Hello," I answered.

"Good evening, cousin," Cohen replied, his voice low and sinister. "Oh wait, I guess I should say morning now."

My hands clenched with pent-up rage, and I jumped to my feet. "Where's Nyla?" I demanded.

Cohen laughed. "She's fine. We had a good time tonight. She's passed out in the bedroom right now."

"I want to talk to her!" I shouted, my whole body shaking with anger.

"Don't worry. She'll be home first thing in the morning. But I have to say, you shocked me tonight."

I was so furious I couldn't see straight. "What the hell are you talking about?"

Cohen chuckled. "I received some pictures of you and a sultry blonde looking mighty cozy in a parking lot."

I froze in place, my gut clenching so hard I could feel it twisting inside of me. I should've known Cohen would do anything to come between me and Nyla.

"You son of a bitch," I growled in disgust. "You had me followed."

"Hey, I just want Nyla to know she might not be

able to trust you. She leaves for one day and you're off with another woman."

Running a hand through my hair, I stormed across the living room floor. "You set this whole thing up. You paid the woman to come onto me, didn't you?"

Cohen snorted. "Do you seriously think I would do something like that?"

"I know you would," I snapped. "You can't have Nyla, so you'll do anything to break us apart."

Cohen laughed. "I can't have Nyla? That's not what she said a couple of hours ago when I put a ring on her finger."

Anger consumed me further. "What the hell are you trying to do?"

He laughed again. "Don't worry, cousin. The story should be on the internet soon. I'm sure everyone in town will be talking about it first thing in the morning."

"Where's Nyla?" I demanded again. "I want to talk to her!"

"Sorry," Cohen replied, "that's not going to happen tonight."

The line went dead, and I slammed my phone onto the kitchen counter.

What was I going to do?

My heart thundered in my chest as I looked over at the clock on the wall. An idea came to mind, but I didn't know if it'd work. Still, I had to try.

SITTING outside the Sandy Shore Bed & Breakfast was a ludicrous idea, but it was precisely what I did.

Was Candace speaking the truth when she said she was staying there? Maybe, maybe not.

Either way, I had to try to find her. And if she was staying there, she had to leave at some point.

I watched the entrance of the two-story brick building, parked only a few blocks down the quaint downtown streets. The sun had just risen over the horizon when Candace emerged from the bed and breakfast, dressed in running shorts and a tank top, with her blonde hair pulled high in a ponytail. She took off down the sidewalk with earbuds in her ears, her mouth moving along with the music. It wasn't my plan to chase after her, but I didn't know what else to do; I had to get answers.

Once out of my car, I ran across the street. Candace was still a few yards ahead of me, but I didn't want to frighten her. A break in the sidewalk was coming up, and I knew she would have to stop before running to the other side. When she did, I took that as my opportunity.

"Candace!" I called out.

She jerked around and a smile lit up her face as she took out her earbuds. "Hey, you. Did you decide to take me up on my offer?"

"No," I said, peering around at our surroundings for photographers.

It made me wonder if Cohen still had people following me. I turned my focus back to Candace, my gaze penetrating hers.

"How do you know Cohen Sumner?"

Her smile dropped instantly, and she shook her head. "I have no clue who that is."

She tried to walk away, but I kept up with her. "Yes, you do," I claimed, refusing to back down. "He hired you to sabotage me. And it's not the first time he's done it either. You did this to me once before, many years ago."

Her eyes widened and she froze, mouth gaping in shock. "You remember me?"

It was those words that confirmed everything.

My hands started to shake, but I clenched them tight. "I thought you looked familiar last night, but I didn't know for sure until now."

Cohen had lied from the very beginning. He didn't just try breaking me and Nyla up now, but he'd also tried it several years ago. Our rivalry ran deeper than I ever could've imagined. What infuriated me was that Cohen knew Nyla was mine back then—*lying bastard*.

"It was years ago," I began, watching Candace fidget nervously with her fingernails. "You wanted my help with a flat tire, and afterward, you tried to make your move, but you and the photographers didn't get the kiss you wanted at the end."

Candace threw her arms in the air. "Okay, my acting sucked back then, and my timing was off. You got me. I owed Cohen some favors after he helped me get an acting gig."

"So, Cohen paid you to come between me and Nyla. Not once, but twice."

She shrugged flippantly like it didn't bother her that she could've helped ruin a real, true relationship.

"It didn't work then, and I doubt it worked last night," she said, rolling her eyes. "That's probably why he took matters into his own hands."

I didn't like the sound of that.

"What do you mean?"

She shook her head and laughed. "You and everyone else in this tiny little town are so clueless. It's kind of cute how slow everything is here." Her gaze shifted to my pocket where I had my phone. "Your precious doctor and Cohen got engaged last night. It's all over the internet." She batted her eyelashes impatiently. "If you don't believe me, look it up. It'll be the first thing that pops up."

I dreaded looking online because I knew it was what Cohen wanted me to do; he'd said there would be a story. But of course, no matter how much I resisted, curiosity got the best of me.

My fingers trembled as I pulled out my phone

and tapped the screen. As soon as Cohen's name was in the search bar, the first article that popped up was of his engagement—to none other than Nyla Clark. My breath caught in my throat when I saw the photo. He was on one knee, a diamond ring glimmering in his hands as he slid it onto her finger.

"That thing has to be worth half a million dollars; it's huge. There's no way she'd say no to that," Candace said from behind me, her voice almost jealous.

Heart pounding, I looked away from my phone. "What did Cohen tell you about this whole situation?"

Candace huffed as if I was annoying her with my questions. "Not that I really care what Cohen does with his personal life, but he bought out some surf shop down here to give him a reason to stay in town. He knew Nyla was here."

It was one thing to make my life miserable but another to involve Nyla; she had nothing to do with our family feud.

"Why did he bring Nyla into all of this? If he's dead set on making my life miserable, he could've done it a million other ways instead of involving her."

Candace shook her head. "No, he wanted Nyla. He saw her with you at some family reunion a long time ago. Ever since then, he was intrigued by her."

That piece of shit had lied to Nyla from the very

beginning. He's always known that she was my ex-wife.

Candace stepped closer to me and glanced at my phone. "I don't even know why he's so hung up on her; she's not good enough for him."

My eyes narrowed at her words, and I snapped back. "*He's* the one who's not good for *her.*"

Candace rolled her eyes and hopped on her feet, ready to get back to running again. "Cohen forks out a lot of money to pay people to do many things for him. He always gets what he wants."

Fury rose inside me and my knuckles turned white as I held onto my phone. "Yeah, well, not this time."

Turning away from Candace, I marched quickly back to my car and once inside, I started typing out numerous texts to Nyla explaining everything I had just found out.

I only hoped she read them in time.

29

NYLA

Cohen's driver showed up right at six. Even though I didn't sleep a wink, I stayed in the room the entire night. I didn't want to speak to Cohen or see his face after everything that had happened.

Throughout the night, I tried calling Miles no less than a hundred times. I didn't have my phone charger, so after a while I stopped to preserve my battery.

Once five o'clock rolled around, I sat by the window and waited for the limo to drive down the driveway. I was downstairs and out the door as soon as it came into view.

Cohen was right behind me and said good morning, but I ignored him and got in the limo. The car ride to the airport was silent, the tension so thick I could barely breathe. If it didn't take a five-hour drive to get back to Oak Island, I would've rented a car. I needed to get back as fast as possible.

Every so often I checked my phone, but there was still no signal, which made no sense. I've never had such horrible cell reception.

We pulled up to the tarmac where Cohen's white jet waited on us, its engines running. As Cohen exited the car and extended a hand to me, I got out on my own and squared my shoulders before marching toward the plane. Before I could take a step up onto the stairs, Cohen blocked my way.

"Are you seriously going to give me the silent treatment the whole way back?" His green eyes were full of anger and disappointment.

"I don't know what to say, Cohen. When we get back to Oak Island, it's going to be a mess. Miles isn't going to let this go. I hoped you two could work things out, but it won't be possible now."

Cohen scoffed, his expression full of disdain. I'd never seen him look like that before. "That's never going to be possible, Nyla."

I threw my hands up in the air. "Why? Why can't you two stop hating each other and move on?"

Cohen shook his head. "Because he has you now. He's the reason why you're not mine. Everything would've worked out if he hadn't gotten in the way."

I was done.

I didn't want to hear anymore.

Brushing past him, I climbed into the cabin of the

jet and took a seat at the very back. After a few minutes, Cohen settled himself in one of the front seats but stayed silent throughout the flight. I pulled out my phone and there was still no cell service.

All I could think about was Miles; I hoped he could trust me. One thing I knew for sure: it certainly didn't look good being gone all night with another man.

ONCE THE PLANE landed and we were in Cohen's car, his phone started to ding with incoming messages. I kept waiting for mine to do the same.

Then, finally, I could hear the vibrations from it in my purse. I was about to reach in and grab it, but Cohen pulled over to the side of the road.

"You need to see these," he said, holding out his phone.

Huffing, I took it and looked at the picture on his screen. It was of Miles and a beautiful blonde with her arms wrapped around him, kissing him. They were in The Beachcomber parking lot. There were more of them together, all with her smiling and touching him, but there were none where I could see his face. It seemed a little too convenient. Anger poured through me, but it wasn't directed at Miles. Cohen may have duped me before, but I wasn't about to let him get in my head. It wasn't a coincidence that there was someone taking pictures of Miles. He would never jeopardize what we had.

"Why were you following him?" I snapped, setting his phone in the center console.

I didn't want to see anymore.

Cohen huffed and pulled back onto the road. "Because he's not worthy of you. Look at what he does when he knows you're off with another guy."

I laughed, but there was no humor to it. When I turned to him, it was as if I could finally see through him.

"Or he was set up," I fired back. "I know you have connections, Cohen. Who's to say you didn't set that whole thing up just like you did with us at your cabin? I'm not going to believe anything you show me." I clenched my jaw and gestured toward the road ahead of us. "Just take me home. I have to get ready for work."

We weren't far from my house, but I could hear my phone vibrating every few seconds. I grabbed it out of my purse, and there were so many missed texts from Miles. As I read his urgent messages, realization slowly set in.

Miles: I know you can't call because that cocksucker is blocking you.

Miles: Please don't listen to anything he's telling you.

> Miles: I hope this gets to you before it's too late.

> Miles: I was set up and I have proof. The pictures of me and Candace are not what it seems. Cohen paid her to come onto me.

> Miles: Cohen bought out Freddy's so that he could get close to you. He knew you were in Oak Island.

> Miles: He tried sabotaging our relationship a long time ago too.

> Miles: HE'S ALWAYS KNOWN WHO YOU WERE.

> Miles: Just know I love you and I hope you trust me.

My stomach clenched into a tight knot as if a rock had plummeted inside of me, and when I read those fateful words: *He's always known who you were,* it felt as if the blood had drained from my face.

When I met Cohen, he knew I was Miles's ex-wife.

He knew everything about me.

Bile rose up my throat, and I knew I had to get out of the car. My knuckles whitened as I leaned forward in my seat and clenched my hand around the door handle. We were just around the corner from my house, but I couldn't risk Cohen showing up there with Miles around; it would be a disaster.

"Pull over!" I shouted.

The second Cohen stopped the car, I yanked open the door and stumbled out, nearly dropping my purse on the asphalt.

"Nyla, what's wrong?" Cohen asked, his voice laced with confusion.

Just hearing him speak made me clench my teeth until they ached.

"Everything!" I seethed, throwing my arms wide and spinning around to face him. "You are such a liar!"

His brows furrowed. "About what?"

The audacity to play dumb just astounded me. Did he really think I wouldn't find out?

"You knew who I was before you even came to Oak Island," I spat out. "Freddy's was just an excuse for you to come here and make your move on me."

He opened his mouth as if to deny it, but when our eyes met, I could finally see the truth written all over his face. Everything seemed to click into place at that moment, spilling through me like liquid fire.

Cohen walked around the side of his car, leaning against it casually as if he was posing for a photo shoot. "If you want the truth, I'll give it to you," he said coolly. "I've been waiting for an opportunity to get close to you. Many years ago, I saw you at one of our family reunions. You were standing alone, and I was going to speak to you, but then Miles came to your side."

I held up my phone. "Miles texted me. You paid that Candace woman to come onto him. And you tried to ruin our marriage years ago, too. Don't even try to deny it."

Cohen held up his hands in defeat. "Fine, I don't deny it. Yes, I tried breaking you two up once before. It didn't work. I got lucky when you two destroyed it yourselves. I tried finding ways to get into your life when I found out."

It had all been a game from the beginning, dating back all those years ago. I had only been to one of Miles's family reunions where his entire family was in attendance, and that was eight years ago.

The thought of Cohen devising a plan for that long didn't seem real.

I rubbed a hand over my aching chest; the deception ran deep.

"Was this all a game to you?" I asked, trying to control my anger. "Did you only want me so you could torture Miles?"

Cohen averted his gaze briefly to the ground, then lifted it to mine. "Yes and no." He pushed off his car and stepped toward me. "I wanted you the second I saw you, Nyla. Knowing it would hurt Miles made it even better when I pursued you. But then I got to know you and I fell hard. My plan backfired on me."

He tried to move closer, but I held up a hand, halting him. Pain flashed across his face, but I didn't know if it was genuine or not. All he'd mostly done was lie to me.

"I feel sorry for you, Cohen. I hate that this jealousy between you and Miles has turned you into whatever you are," I said, waving a hand about his body. "I thought I saw some redeeming qualities in you, unless every moment you spent with me was a lie."

Cohen shook his head. "It wasn't all a lie, Nyla. I do have feelings for you, and I would've married you in a heartbeat." He placed a hand over his heart. "I'm in love with you."

I wanted to believe that was true, that he *could* love someone. Sadly, I didn't think he was capable, at least not until he turned his life around. Being deceitful and manipulative would not make him happy for the rest of his life.

Slowly, I breathed in the salty sea air and released it. "As angry as I am with you right now, I do hope you are able to find real love one day. Honestly, I think it'll help you become a better man. Because right now, I'm not seeing it." A fleeting expression of pain crossed Cohen's face again before quickly disappearing behind a carefully crafted mask of indifference. "Then again," I continued. "A part of me wants to punch the dog shit out of you, but I'm afraid I'll break my hand."

Cohen laughed once and nodded. "That's the Nyla I fell for. I deserve anything you throw my way." He lowered his gaze and blew out a sigh. "Will I ever see you again?"

I waited for him to meet my gaze again before answering. "No," I replied, wanting him to see all the emotions on my face. "Our relationship ends here. I don't think I can ever forgive you for this, and I know Miles never will." My house was only around the corner, so I nodded at his car. "You can leave now. I'm going to walk the rest of the way."

I was about to pick my purse up off the ground, but then I looked at my hand and smiled. There was only one way to let go of my anger. Cohen turned his back on me to walk to his side of the car, but I closed the distance quickly.

"Hey," I shouted, catching him off guard. The second he turned around, I punched the right side of his face. It felt like fire shooting up my arm, but knowing I punished him a little felt good. He grunted in pain and stumbled back into his car, lifting a hand to his face. "Okay, I deserve that," he said, moving his jaw back and forth.

Adrenaline coursed through my veins, and I knew once it wore off, my hand would hurt much worse than it did now. "Yes, you did. Goodbye, Cohen. You might want to leave town before Miles finds you."

I didn't bother watching him drive away; instead, I made my way home. When I was about to reach the driveway, Miles sprinted out of the house. He caught me in his arms and spun me around, planting his lips on mine in a passionate kiss.

"I was so worried about you. Are you all right?" he asked as he put me down on my feet again.

"I'm so sorry for ever trusting Cohen. You were right about everything."

A low growl rumbled in his chest. "Where is he?" he demanded.

"He's gone," I said. "But I left him a parting gift."

I let him go and he cupped my cheeks, his eyes searching mine. "What do you mean?" My hand had already started to swell up, and I could feel it throbbing. I held it up so he could see the damage and his eyes widened. "He's going to have a black eye. My hand hurts like hell."

Miles chuckled before kissing it gently. "I hate I didn't get to see it." He dangled an arm over my shoulders as we walked inside the house together.

"I have to get ready for work. I'm going to need a lot of coffee this morning."

The second I stepped into the kitchen, it smelled like coffee heaven. Miles had a fresh pot brewed for us.

"I got you covered," he said. "I have a class to teach at the Cape Fear station. I didn't want to leave without knowing you were okay."

I glanced over at the clock, and luckily, I still had a few minutes left to get ready for work. "I hate that we went through everything last night only to spend the day apart. But I promise, tonight is all ours. It's time we start planning our future."

Miles stepped closer and pulled me into his embrace. His gaze never left mine as he spoke, and a smirk spread across his face. "Looks like we have a few minutes before we both have to be at work."

My heart raced with anticipation, and I couldn't help but smile. "Yeah, and?" I asked, hoping we had the same thing on our minds.

He swept me off my feet and carried me down the hall to our bedroom. Reaching out with one arm, he dropped me onto the mattress and followed closely behind. His kiss was full of passion and I deepened it, loving how he held me protectively in his arms.

"I think I need to show you how much I love you," he said, his breath warm against my neck.

I melted into him and smiled. "Be my guest."

The day had gone by quickly and I was exhausted. I filled Autumn and Gina in on everything that had happened. Even Everleigh came by the office at lunch, and we talked the entire time. I didn't want to leave the office and go anywhere in town because I knew everyone was talking about the tabloids. News sure did travel fast in the entertainment world. Nothing had gotten out of hand yet, but I had a feeling it was about to.

The world knew my name and where I lived, courtesy of Cohen and his attempts to hurt Miles. Cohen knew I didn't want to be in the public eye, but he made sure I had no choice or say in the matter. It was like the calm before the storm. I had a feeling Miles knew it, too. Even the clouds in the sky felt ominous, all thick and gray with the sound of thunder in the distance.

The sand was warm beneath my feet as we walked down the beach. It was summer and crowded, and I could feel eyes on us.

"I'm starting to think we should've stayed behind closed doors," I said, keeping my voice low.

I glanced around at the people milling about and noticed several of them had their phones out, capturing us on camera. I released a nervous breath and tightened my grip on Miles's hand.

Miles sighed and kept walking. "It is what it is, sunshine. We can't hide forever. Knowing Cohen, this isn't over."

It sounded as if there was an underlying threat behind his words. I looked up at him and squeezed his hand.

"Please tell me you're not going to go after him."

Miles's jaw clenched and he reluctantly met my gaze. "I can't let it go, Nyla. You got your last words in, but I haven't. What he did to us was wrong."

My chest tightened with dread. "What are you going to do?"

He shrugged and averted his gaze. "I don't know yet. Today, Jensen told me that he ran into Cohen at Freddy's. Apparently, he's planning on leaving for New York first thing tomorrow. I was thinking of paying him a visit."

I couldn't blame him for wanting to confront Cohen. However, the last thing I wanted was for Miles to get charged with assault. With everything Cohen was capable of, I wouldn't put it past him to get the police involved—what better way to taint Miles's life than with a police record?

"I can't believe he knew who I was the entire time," I said, still not believing it.

Cohen was a good actor. I didn't like how easily I fell for it; I was too trusting.

Miles's grip tightened on my hand as if he was trying to keep himself from flying off the handle. "Whatever you do, don't blame yourself. He's spent his whole life manipulating people. He's very good at what he does."

We walked barefoot through the sand, our toes sinking into the wet grains. I leaned into Miles's warmth and caught a whiff of his cologne.

"It's kind of sad," I said. "Cohen wasn't born to manipulate and lie. He's a product of his surroundings. I doubt he'll ever find real happiness in his life."

Miles scoffed dismissively. "He doesn't deserve it."

We stopped walking and I stepped in front of him, placing my hands on his chest. His heartbeat thudded against them as I looked up into his eyes.

"Promise me you won't do anything stupid tomorrow when you see him," I pleaded softly.

Miles stared back at me for a few seconds before releasing a long sigh and shaking his head. The breath stalled in my lungs as I waited to hear his next words.

"I can't promise that, Nyla," he said gravely. "I wish you knew how much anger I have in me right now; not being able to let it go is eating me up inside."

Closing my eyes, I blew out the air I'd been holding in my lungs and nodded in reply. "Do what you have to do. I'll support you no matter what."

He kissed me gently, wrapping his arms protectively around me as if shielding me from what was about to come next.

"Don't worry," he whispered against my skin, "I won't kill him." He pulled away and gave me a half-smile. "But I will say that when I couldn't get in touch with you last night, it was one of the worst moments of my life. I had no clue what was going on or if you were okay."

Tears welled up in my eyes. "I was afraid you'd think the worst. The last thing I wanted you to believe was that I was sleeping with Cohen."

Taking both of my hands in his own, Miles kissed each one tenderly before locking his gaze with mine again. "I never thought that. I've always trusted you."

I gently pulled away from him and looked into his eyes. "Same with you, even after seeing those pictures of you and that other woman. They looked scandalous, but I knew you would never hurt me like that."

Miles shook his head and cupped my cheeks. "Never. I love you way too much."

"And I love *you*," I said back. "Always."

We walked hand in hand for a little longer until darkness overtook the sky. Lightning flashed on the horizon, and the sound of thunder rumbled all around us. I was worried about Miles confronting Cohen, but maybe it needed to be done. Cohen already got a black eye from me, but he could definitely use another one.

31

MILES

I screeched to a stop in front of Cohen's house just as he threw the last of his bags into the trunk of his expensive sports car. He didn't even bother turning around. I could feel my heart pounding in my chest as I got out of my car and marched over to him.

"Did you think I was going to let Nyla get the last word in?" I snarled. Cohen huffed and turned around to face me. His right eye was swollen with a deep purple bruise surrounding it; Nyla had hit him hard. "You think you can get away with what you did?" I seethed.

His eyes were cold as he crossed his arms and tilted his head defiantly. "I knew you'd show your face here at some point. What you're not going to get is an apology from me. I'm not sorry for anything I did."

Fury ripped through me and my fists clenched at my side. "You tried sabotaging my marriage years ago, asshole! What the hell is wrong with you? Where in your messed up brain would you ever think that's okay?"

Cohen shrugged, his expression disinterested. "I know what I want, and I was going to do anything to get it."

I shook my head in disgust. "You keep playing these games, trying to get what you want, but you never win. Just take a look at your face right now."

Cohen's glare intensified, but I didn't back down. "Get out of here, Miles," he spat.

I balled my hands into tight fists, rage coursing through my veins as I stepped forward. Cohen tried to turn away, but I grabbed his collar and shoved him against his car. His eyes widened in surprise, then quickly clouded with anger. He grabbed my wrist and tried to pull me away, but I held him in an iron grip.

"I'm not going anywhere until you say you're not going to bother me or Nyla again."

His face contorted into a sneer of defiance. "Get the hell off me!"

"Say it!" I shouted, tightening my hold on his wrist.

He stared at me for a long moment before throwing up his arms in surrender, breaking out of my hold. "Dammit, I'm leaving. I don't plan on coming back to this small ass town again. I'm not going to waste my time on you or her."

I shoved him away and he staggered back against his car, head bouncing off the metal frame.

"Good. Now get out of here. I don't ever want to see you again. And if you try any more bullshit, I'll fly right up to New York and make you regret it."

But, of course, Cohen still wasn't done goading me. A sly smirk spread across his face as he straightened his shirt.

"You say I lost, but how does it feel to know I had your wife?" He raised an eyebrow in challenge and his grin grew wider. "For a whole month, she was mine."

My vision blurred with red as fury surged within me and without another thought, my right arm flew forward and connected with Cohen's jaw before he could even blink. His head snapped back from the force of the impact, and he stumbled backward, trying to catch himself but failing as he tumbled to the ground. He groaned in pain as he lay there motionless, then slowly rose to his feet with a menacing glare that promised retribution.

"She was never yours," I growled through gritted teeth, pointing an accusing finger at him. "She's always been mine."

With those final words, I got in my car and left, happy that I had given him a parting gift. His left eye was going to match his right.

32

NYLA

3 WEEKS LATER

S o much had happened in the past three weeks. First, Freddy bought back his surf shop from Cohen, which was a relief because we knew Cohen wouldn't have a reason to return since he didn't own it anymore.

The paparazzi had a field day with everything that had happened. It was called a scandalous love triangle between New York's most eligible bachelor, the small-town doctor who captured his heart, and the jealous cousin who stole her away.

A couple of weeks ago, I felt like I was in the calm before the storm; I was right. One of the things I didn't want from being in a relationship with Cohen was the craziness of the paparazzi. Let me tell you . . . it got wild and absolutely ridiculous.

Miles and I had just one night of peace before everything blew up around us. Reporters pretended to be sick so they could get an appointment with me at the clinic. They wanted my side of the story, but I didn't care to elaborate. So, instead, the tabloids made Cohen seem like a victim of a broken heart, which was fine with me. All that mattered was that I knew the truth. Miles and I had to deal with the mess for about two weeks. Thankfully, the paparazzi grew somewhat bored with us when they realized no other scandalous things were going on.

However, on the other hand, Cohen didn't suffer at all. He got the attention he wanted and was reaping the benefits. I saw a video clip on the internet of him walking through Times Square, and so many women were throwing themselves at him, saying they could heal his heart. Unfortunately, Miles and I were viewed as the villains.

"Want another piece of cake?" Miles asked, chuckling lightly as I scooped the last bite onto my fork and devoured it.

Even though I probably could've eaten another piece, I knew I shouldn't. One of the things I loved about attending weddings was the cake. I slid my plate to the side and pursed my lips at him. Miles was extremely good-looking in his tux with his blond hair perfectly coifed. I'd watched him stand with Luke as he said his wedding vows to his new bride; it brought back so many memories of my wedding day.

"No, I'm good. Might as well leave some for other people."

Miles clutched my hand and brought it to his lips, kissing it softly. "Want to dance?"

The dance floor was filled with people, all swaying slowly to a Hadley Rivers country song. He winked at me and smiled.

"Seems fitting since we have a history with Hadley Rivers."

I laughed. "Yes, we do."

I looked at all the people and focused on his parents, staring at each other as if they were the only two people in the world. They've been married for forty-five years and still going strong.

"It's been nice seeing your parents again," I said, clutching his hand. "I used to love talking to your mom."

Miles kissed the top of my head. "She loves talking to you, too. And just so you know, my parents are thinking of visiting us soon. They want to see Oak Island."

That made me smile. "Anytime."

The song was almost halfway done, but before I could stand and pull him to the dance floor, two teenage girls rushed over to us, holding what looked to be tabloid magazines in their hands. One of the girls had long blonde hair and braces, while the other had shorter brown hair and glasses.

The blonde held out the magazine along with a black marker. "Can we please have your autographs?"

My mouth dropped and I had no choice but to take the magazine from her. The other girl handed her magazine to Miles. On the cover was a picture of Cohen, Miles, and me with the headline: *The Choice Has Been Made.* Then under that, the subtitle was: *New York's Famous Bachelor is Now Single Again.*

Miles narrowed his gaze at them, his lips pulling back in a sly grin. "Before we sign these, do you think we're the bad guys in the story?"

The blonde snorted and shook her head. "Definitely, not. Anyone can see that Cohen guy is a jerk."

I signed my name underneath my picture on both magazines and Miles did the same. The blonde gasped and opened the magazine, sliding it to where I could see.

"I don't know if you've read this or not, but Hollywood is thinking of making a movie about you guys. Won't that just be epic?"

Miles and I turned to each other, and his shoulders shook with laughter. "I wonder who they'd get to play me?"

The girls looked at each other and snickered, but

the brown-haired girl was the one who spoke up first. "I'd say, Chris Hemsworth."

The blonde shook her head. "No, Ryan Gosling."

My eyes widened, and I laughed when Miles sat back, grinning triumphantly. "Girls, you're going to make Miles get a big head."

Miles threw his arms up in the air. "What are you saying? Do I not look as hot as those guys?" The girls giggled and walked away, leaving me alone with him.

Leaning in close, I nipped his ear playfully and whispered. "You are way sexier than them, sweetheart."

"You expect me to believe that?"

I moved back and shrugged; there was no doubt in my mind. "It's the truth."

The music faded to silence, and an expectant hush filled the crowded hall. The bride, radiant in her white gown with her dark curls woven into a ball of cascading flowers, stepped up onto the stage and surveyed the guests. She grinned mischievously and held the bouquet of rainbow-hued blossoms high over her head.

"All righty, ladies!" Her voice echoed across the room. "Who wants to catch the bouquet?"

A chorus of squeals erupted from the single women around me, and they began to sprint toward an empty patch of the dance floor at the center of the room.

Miles nudged me in the ribs with his elbow. "You better get out there. You're not married."

"No, but I was before," I said, dreading the thought of joining the crowd of crazy women who looked as if they'd scratch my eyes out if I caught the bouquet. "That should count me as being ineligible."

I glanced over my shoulder at his mother, who was beckoning me with a wide smile. With a sigh, I reluctantly joined the other eager single ladies on the floor.

Kristina spun around so her back was to us and shouted, "On three! One! Two! Three!"

As I watched her swing her arm back to throw, I told myself I wouldn't even attempt to reach for them. But as I watched the flowers sail through the air straight toward me, I had no choice but to catch them before they hit me in the head. The crowd cheered, but there were a few scowls from the women around me. Luckily, the music started up again and Miles came to my side. He pulled me into him and kissed me.

"It must be a sign," he said, nodding at the flowers.

I wrapped my arms around his neck. "I was wondering if you were ever going to ask me to marry you again."

A mischievous twinkle sparkled in his eyes. "Do you still have your rings?"

It just so happened that I did, hidden away in a small jewelry box in my pajama drawer.

"I do," I replied. "You?"

Miles nodded, his expression serious. "Tucked away for when I needed it again. I was hoping one day I would."

My heart raced and I cupped his cheek. "How about you get it out and we try this whole marriage thing again?"

Miles held me tighter, his eyes full of longing. "Is that what you want?"

There was no hesitation.

"Yes. More than anything. I don't need a fancy wedding; I just need you."

My eyes started to burn when Miles rested his forehead on mine. "Think it'll work this time?"

Our lips touched and I breathed him in. "I know it will."

33

NYLA

AUGUST

Our August wedding was perfect. I couldn't have asked for a better day. The sun shone brightly overhead all day, and the temperature hovered around eighty degrees. The ceremony was small with just our parents and close friends attending: no extended family. Although, we had no doubt word had spread to Cohen of our nuptials. Luckily, he didn't try to contact us. I was pretty sure he was gone for good from our lives.

Everleigh was my matron of honor and Luke stood by Miles as his best man, just like he did before at our first wedding. Since Everleigh got married in her backyard by the beach and it was so beautiful, I took her idea and did the same.

Miles and I said our vows in front of the big oak tree in our backyard with the Intracoastal Waterway as the perfect backdrop. My dress was simple, just a silky off-white gown that gently hugged my body.

Now that everyone had left, I changed out of my dress into shorts and a tank top and sat on the dock, enjoying the last rays of sunshine shimmering across the water. I lifted my hand and smiled as my engagement ring sparkled.

"If you wanted a new ring, I would've gotten you one," Miles said from behind me. I didn't even hear him walk across the dock. "I did sell my house in Virginia, which gave us quite an impressive sum of money."

This was true. We had a lot of money in the bank and it was lovely. He'd also taken a job at the local fire station. For once, everything was finally coming together perfectly.

Miles sat beside me and handed me a glass of wine, even though I was still full from our exquisite dinner, catered by The Beachcomber, and our delicious wedding cake. I couldn't have asked for a better day.

Miles moved closer so I rested my head on his shoulder. "My ring is perfect," I whispered, staring down at it. It was a small diamond, but that didn't matter to me. All that mattered was that Miles was mine again. I lifted my face to his and kissed him. "I wouldn't trade it in for anything else."

The diamond on my finger sparkled in the dim light as I took a sip of my wine and closed my eyes to savor the heady flavor that lingered on my tongue. I opened my eyes and set the glass down on the dock beside us before curling up in Miles's lap. He chuckled and gently brushed an errant strand of hair away from my face.

"Are you ready to start our honeymoon now?" he asked, gazing into my eyes.

In just a few short hours, we were going to be on a plane to the Maldives. It was a place we'd always wanted to go to but never could afford it. I felt my heart flutter as I wrapped my arms around Miles's neck and smiled at him.

"I'm down for that. Then, afterward, I might have to snag another piece of wedding cake." It was lemon flavored with buttercream icing, the perfect combination.

Miles laughed and shook his head. "You're not going to try sneaking some in your luggage, are you?"

That thought hadn't escaped my mind, but I didn't want to ruin a perfectly good cake.

I rolled my eyes and chuckled. "No way! I'm going to wrap the rest up really well and pray that it lasts until we get back from our honeymoon."

Warmth flooded through me as Miles looked

deep into my eyes. "I can't believe I can call you my wife again."

My heart soared at his words. "It feels surreal. Sometimes when I think back to our past, it's almost as if it was just a dream. But I will never forget how I felt when you first proposed to me."

A wave of nostalgia hit me as I remembered that day.

Miles chuckled and rested his hands on my hips. "Ah, yes, that was an unforgettable day. I was so afraid I was going to lose the ring on the trail."

At that time, we were both so young and full of love. Miles had taken me on a hike and as we reached the summit, he got down on one knee and proposed to me with the same ring I had on today. I had no hesitation in saying yes. The level of happiness I felt that day was off the charts.

Miles's hands moved slowly down my hips, and the sheer intensity of his gaze caused me to tremble.

"I have a question," I said, my voice just above a whisper.

Miles lifted his eyebrows in response. "What?"

I bit my lip, trying to contain my grin. "Now that Everleigh and Jensen have had their son, she's been asking when we plan on having our own kids." His eyes drifted down to my lips as I spoke, and I felt a warmth radiating between us. Clearing my throat, I continued. "If we have a boy, they could be best friends."

Miles locked his gaze with mine again. "And if we have a girl?"

A smile stretched across my face at the thought. "Then maybe they'll be childhood friends and get married one day," I replied, shrugging playfully.

He chuckled lightly. "No boy is ever going to be good enough for my daughter," he said with a smirk. "Even if it is Jensen and Everleigh's son."

We both laughed and I could just imagine how much hell he was going to give the boys when they came around if we had a daughter.

Miles tenderly cupped my face between his strong hands and pressed his lips firmly against mine. "I'm ready to start a family with you, Nyla," he whispered, resting his forehead on mine. "I've been ready."

Tears streamed down my cheeks as I smiled. "Then what are we waiting for?"

The next step of our lives was about to happen . . . and I couldn't wait for it to begin.

THE END

ABOUT THE AUTHOR

New York Times and *USA Today* bestselling author L. P. Dover is a southern belle living in North Carolina with her husband and two beautiful girls. Everything's sweeter in the South has always been her mantra and she lives by it, whether it's with her writing or in her everyday life. Maybe that's why she's seriously addicted to chocolate.

Dover has written countless novels in several different genres, including a children's book with her daughter. Her favorite to write is romantic suspense, but she's also found a passion in romantic comedy. She loves to make people laugh which is why you'll never see her without a smile on her face.

You can find L.P. Dover at www.lpdover.com.

ALSO BY L.P. DOVER

SECOND CHANCES SERIES

Love's Second Chance

Trusting You

What He Wants (Trusting You Prequel)

Meant for Me

Fighting for Love

Intercepting Love

Catching Summer

Defending Hayden

Last Chance

Intended for Bristol

ARMED & DANGEROUS SERIES

No Limit

Roped In

High-Sided

CIRCLE OF JUSTICE SERIES

Trigger

Target

Aim

In the Crossfire

ARMED & DANGEROUS/CIRCLE OF JUSTICE CROSSOVER SERIES

Dangerous Game

Dangerous Betrayals

Book 3 - TBD

Book 4 – TBD

GLOVES OFF SERIES

A Fighter's Desire – Part One

A Fighter's Desire – Part Two

Tyler's Undoing

Ryley's Revenge

Winter Kiss: Ryley and Ash

Paxton's Promise

Camden's Redemption

Kyle's Return

GLOVES OFF - NEXT GENERATION SERIES

Craving the Fight

Taking the Fight

Wanting the Fight

Desiring the Fight

Longing for the Fight

Loving the Fight

Needing the Fight

Ending the Fight

SOCIETY X SERIES W/HEIDI MCLAUGHLIN

Dark Room

Viewing Room

Play Room

FOREVER FAE SERIES

Forever Fae

Betrayals of Spring

Summer of Frost

Reign of Ice

LAND OF THE FAE SERIES

Winter of the Shadow Fae

Spring of the Cursed Fae

Summer of the Siren Fae

TBA

TBA

ROYAL SHIFTERS SERIES

Turn of the Moon

Resisting the Moon

Rise of the Moon

Unleashed by the Moon

Bound by the Moon

Claimed by the Moon

Taken Under the Moon

Awakened by the Moon

BREAKAWAY SERIES

Hard Stick

Blocked

Playmaker

Off the Ice

STANDALONE NOVELS

The Truth About Secrets

Love, Lies & Deception

Going for the Hole

Anonymous

Love, Again

Fairytale Confessions

THE DATING SERIES W/HEIDI MCLAUGHLIN

A Date for New Year's

A Date with an Admirer

A Date for Good Luck

A Date for the Hunt

A Date for Good Luck

A Date for the Derby

A Date to Play Fore

A Date with a Foodie

A Date for the Fair

A Date for the Regatta

A Date for the Masquerade

A Date with a Turkey

A Date with an Elf

CHRISTMAS NOVELS

It Must've Been the Mistletoe

Snowflake Lane Inn

Christmas With You

MOONLIGHT AND ALEENA SERIES W/ANNA-GRACE DOVER

Moonlight and Aleena: A Tale of Two Friends

OAK ISLAND SERIES

Made in the USA
Middletown, DE
29 August 2023